Lenhard, Elizabeth

Four dragons

The Four Dragons

Adapted by ELIZABETH LENHARD

VOLO

an imprint of
HYPERION BOOKS FOR CHILDREN
New York

For information address Volo Books, 114 Fifth Avenue, New York, New York 10011-5690.

Printed in the United States of America
First Edition
1 3 5 7 9 10 8 6 4 2

This book is set in 12/16.5 Hiroshige Book.

ISBN 0-7868-1798-4

Visit www.clubwitch.com

"JINGLE BELLS . . ."
THE SILVER DRAGON
"JINGLE BELLS . . ."
"JINGLE
ALL THE WAY. . ."
I'M COMING!
ARE YOU STILL IN YOUR ROOM? WE'RE GOING TO BE SUPER LATE!
". . . OH, WHAT FUN IT IS TO RIDE IN A ONE-HORSE, OPEN SLEIGH . . ."
JUST A SEC, IRMA! I'VE ALMOST GOT IT.
YES! HERE'S THAT PICTURE I DREW OF MRS. KNICKERBOCKER. I PROMISED I'D GIVE IT TO HER.
DID YOU HIDE IT UNDER YOUR BED BECAUSE YOU WERE AFRAID SOMEONE WOULD STEAL IT, OR ARE YOU JUST THAT DISORGANIZED? COME ON, HAY LIN! LET'S GET GOING!

DO YOU THINK I'M DISORGANIZED?
IF NOT, THEN SOMEBODY ELSE MUST HAVE SET A FIREWORK OFF IN YOUR LOCKER! IF YOU WANT, I COULD ASK MY DAD FOR HELP. MAYBE HE CAN INVESTIGATE AND FIND OUT WHO DID IT. . . .
WE WASTED HALF AN HOUR FINDING YOUR MASTERPIECE! IF WE ARE LATE FOR SCHOOL, I'M GOING TO BE MAD!
HEY! IT'S NOT LATE AT ALL. . . .
FOTO
HEATHERFIELD NEWS
FRIGID WEATHER STRIKES HEATHERFIELD.
CHRISTMAS DAY TO RECORD SUB-ZERO TEMPERATURES.
SPECIAL FORCES ON THE ALERT.
SINCE WHEN HAVE YOU WANTED TO HURRY TO SCHOOL? DO YOU REALIZE WE'LL BE GETTING THERE EARLY?
SO? WHAT'S WRONG WITH THAT? WE'RE ALWAYS LATE. TODAY WE'LL BE MAKING UP FOR IT!
THERE'S SOMETHING YOU'RE NOT TELLING ME! YOU'VE GOT A DATE, DON'T YOU? YOU'VE GOT A DATE! ADMIT IT!
QUIET DOWN, FOR CRYING OUT LOUD!
EXCUSE ME? IRMA'S GOT A DATE?
NO WAY! WHO'S THE UNLUCKY GUY?
ZIP IT, CORNELIA!
OOOOH! LOOKS LIKE SOMEBODY GOT UP ON THE WRONG SIDE OF THE BED THIS MORNING!

HEY, HOT STUFF! YOU'RE RIGHT ON TIME TODAY! YOU'VE NEVER BEEN THIS PUNCTUAL BEFORE!
!
GROAN! I'M IN FOR IT NOW!
M—MARTIN? IRMA'S DATING MARTIN? MAYBE I HOULD GET MY EYES HECKED! I'M SEEING THINGS! THIS CAN'T REALLY BE HAPPENING!
DON'T WORRY—SHE'S NOT! MARTIN TUTORS IRMA IN FRENCH FOR HALF AN HOUR BEFORE CLASSES START.
IRMA'S REALLY WORRIED ABOUT PASSING. TO MAKE UP FOR HER BAD GRADES, SHE NEEDS TO GET EXTRA CREDIT BY BEING IN THE HOLIDAY PLAY. . . .
. . . BUT IN ORDER TO GET A PART IN THE PLAY, SHE NEEDS TO PASS HER NEXT FRENCH TEST!
HA-HA-HA! NOW I GET IT!
HAY LIN!

I HOPE YOU HAVE YOU-KNOW-WHAT IN THAT BACKPACK OF YOURS!
OF COURSE I DO, MRS. KNICKERBOCKER!
WOULD YOU ALL EXCUSE ME?
WINK
?
WELL, IT'S NOT PERFECT. . . . THE COLORS . . . QUALITY . . .
LET ME BE THE JUDGE OF THAT!
IT'S REMARKABLE! YOU HAVE A GREAT TALENT, HAY LIN, AND I THINK YOU SHOULD SHARE IT WITH YOUR CLASSMATES.
WHAT DO YOU MEAN?
AS YOU KNOW, THE DRAMA CLASS WILL BE PUTTING ON A HOLIDAY PLAY. OUR SCHOOL HAS A MULTIETHNIC TRADITION, SO . . .
. . . THIS YEAR'S PERFORMANCE WILL BE DEDICATED TO LEGENDS FROM AROUND THE WORLD.
WHAT WOULD I HAVE TO DO?

I'D LIKE TO ENTRUST YOU WITH AN ASIAN LEGEND. YOU'D WRITE THE STORY AND DESIGN THE SETS AND COSTUMES. DO YOU THINK YOU'RE UP FOR IT?
WOW! THIS IS GOING TO BE OUT OF THIS WORLD!
AND SO . . .
TUMP
. . . IT'S HOPELESS. I HAVE TO COME UP WITH SOMETHING BETTER THAN THIS.
WHY DON'T YOU GET SOME SLEEP, INSTEAD? IT'S A BIT LATE TO BE WORKING!
SOMETIMES A GOOD NIGHT'S SLEEP CAN SOLVE A LOT OF PROBLEMS. YOU MIGHT JUST DREAM UP THE PERFECT IDEA!
AN ASIAN LEGEND, MOM! DO YOU KNOW ANY?
OH, YOUR GRANDMA KNEW A LOT OF CHINESE LEGENDS! WHEN I WAS LITTLE, SHE WOULD TELL ME A DIFFERENT ONE EVERY NIGHT!
WHAT WAS YOUR FAVORITE?
THE ONE ABOUT THE FOUR DRAGONS!

YES . . . THE FOUR DRAGONS!
THE SKY . . .
TIME WAS YOUNG, THEN.
GRRROOOWWLL
THERE WERE NO RIVERS OR LAKES. . . . JUST THE GREAT EASTERN SEA.
WOOOSH
THE DRAGONS CHASED EACH OTHER THROUGH THE AIR.
WOOOSH
THE BRAVEST WERE THE RED DRAGON, THE YELLOW DRAGON . . .
. . . THE BLACK DRAGON, AND THE PEARL DRAGON.

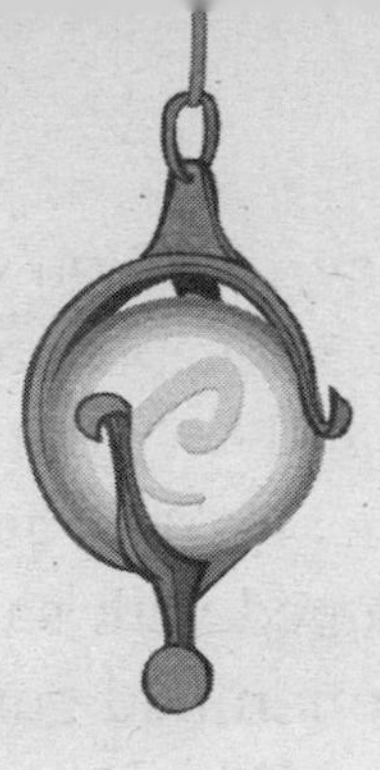

ONE

Hay Lin sat on her bed as her mother got ready to launch into an ancient, Asian tale about four dragons. As she looked at her mother's face, Hay Lin felt the angst that had been eating at her insides begin to ease. She recognized that dreamy expression. It was the same expression her grandmother had often worn on her face. Hay Lin felt an immediate urge to change into pajamas and snuggle under her sheets. She wanted to sink deep into her mother's calming voice. She wanted to feel just like a little kid again.

The idea made Hay Lin sigh with happiness—for a second. In the next second, however, she frowned.

She silently scolded herself: You

don't have time for kid stuff, Hay Lin! You've discovered that a Veil—a bizarre, invisible barrier—exists between earth and a dark, oppressed place called Metamoor. You and your best friends have been charged with saving our world from the Metamoorian bad guys who keep plunging through the Veil. *And,* to make all this saving possible, you've been infused with magical powers.

In other words, you've been given this totally grown-up task. Hay Lin continued to admonish herself silently. This was no time for fairy tales.

And let's face another fact, she thought with a frown. My save-the-world gig isn't the only reason I'm too grown up for these bedtime stories. I mean, I'm practically a teenager. I'm not supposed to like stories and Mom-time.

Hay Lin had trouble picturing her sassy best friend, Irma, cuddling up for a bedtime story with *her* mom. The same went for cool, independent Cornelia. Taranee was too busy going on dates with her cute crush, Nigel, to hang out with her parents. And as for Will? Lately, she and her mom had been fighting like cats and dogs.

Meanwhile, Hay Lin remained cheerfully and lovingly devoted to her family.

And *nobody* knows, Hay Lin brooded further, that I sometimes talk to my grandmother late at night. If they did, I can only imagine their reactions!

Hay Lin's grandmother had passed away a few months ago, but Hay Lin still liked to whisper little jokes and stories to the elderly woman. After all, they had been very close. Somehow, somewhere, Hay Lin was sure her grandmother was listening.

There were even times when Hay Lin thought she could hear her grandmother's wise voice in *her* head.

In fact, Hay Lin felt she could hear her grandmother's voice right *then*, just as her mother got comfortable on the edge of the bed and squeezed Hay Lin's hand.

Perhaps her grandmother's voice was drifting out from Hay Lin's many memories. Or maybe her grandmother really was speaking to her from some ethereal afterworld.

Even if their origin was murky, her grandmother's words were clear: *Don't be in such a hurry to grow up, my little Hay Lin. There's no shame in enjoying a story, at any time of day. Especially when your principal has put you in charge of telling a tale yourself!*

That thought made Hay Lin smile and sit up straight.

Of course, she told herself. Grandma's right. Listening to Mom's tale is research! Mom's simply helping me with homework!

With that thought in her head, Hay Lin hurried over to her dresser and quickly changed into her favorite purple tank top and flannel boxer shorts.

Hay Lin sighed with satisfaction as she moved past her mother to hop into bed.

She grabbed a pad and a pen from her nightstand to take notes. Across the top of the page, she wrote: *The Tale of the Four Dragons*.

Her mother finally began to speak, weaving beautiful images and poetic prose into a rich story.

Only a few sentences into the tale, Hay Lin forgot all about taking notes. She was completely captivated by the beautiful story.

"Once upon a time," Hay Lin's mother began, with a twinkle in her soft, brown eyes, "the sky filled the world. Time was young then. There were no rivers or lakes on earth. Only the great eastern sea. And dragons. Dragons who chased each other through the air."

Immediately, Hay Lin could picture the scene. The air—as pure and blue as spring-water—was filled with gusts of steam and puffs of wind. It was beautiful!

Such airy imagery came naturally to Hay Lin. Each Guardian of the Veil had power over a different element. Cornelia was all about earth. Irma was a water baby. Taranee was friends with fire. And Hay Lin ruled the air. She could flit through the sky as lightly as a leaf and lift the heaviest objects with her own personal gusts of wind.

She could also imagine dragons—sinuous, powerful, and miles long—flying through her sky, without the help of wings. As described by her mother, these wise creatures appeared in four colors.

"Of all the dragons," her mother narrated, "the bravest were the red dragon, the yellow dragon, the black dragon, and the pearl dragon."

According to her mother's description, those

four magnificent beings constantly surveyed the earth. Every day they traveled the globe with effortless grace, gazing down upon its simple beauty—a beauty that was, however, beginning to wither away.

"One sad day," her mother said, "a prayer rose up from earth, carried by the smoke of a thousand sticks of incense. 'Help us, mighty ancestors,' the people begged.

"The yellow dragon," her mother continued, "the one who loved the earth most, swooped down for a closer look. He saw a crowd of people dressed in tattered robes. They were gathered beneath a wizened, leafless tree. The soil beneath their bare feet was cracked and dusty. In the ruthless sun, their hair looked dull and dry, and their faces looked gaunt. They were in dire need of food and water, with strength enough only to cry, 'May the skies open. May the rains return to bless our fields. This is all we hope for. This is what we *beg* for!'

"'Poor people,'" her mother cried, her voice taking on the deep tone of the yellow dragon gazing at the devastation far below. "'The drought is destroying their crops.'

"'Their food is running out,' the red dragon

added. 'Soon it will be the end for them!'

"The yellow dragon shed a tear," her mother continued. "He said, 'Their suffering is great. Let us go seek help from the mighty Jade Emperor!' Immediately, the four dragons flew off toward the heavenly palace where the emperor lived."

"The Jade Emperor," Hay Lin whispered. "Right."

Once again, a vivid picture formed in her mind. She saw an ancient man clad in a claret-colored, silk robe and a superlong, white beard. He was imperious and crabby, even though he lounged upon sumptuous, red cushions and had a servant who sat near him, fanning him. As pots of fragrant incense smoldered at his feet, the emperor glanced grumpily at the four dragons, who knelt respectfully before him.

Her mother continued, "The dragons' welcome was far from pleasant. Arching a silvery eyebrow, the emperor drawled, 'Why have you come here to disturb me? Why couldn't you simply stay among your clouds?'

"It was the red dragon who stepped forward, bowing his mighty head.

"'The people are suffering greatly, Your

Highness,' he said. 'If you do not send rain immediately, it will mean the end for them. They will be destroyed!'"

Hay Lin couldn't help catching her breath as her mother continued to weave the tale. It was a dramatic story. It also felt strangely familiar to her.

"The emperor spoke," her mother said, interrupting Hay Lin's reflection. "'I will see to it,' he said. 'Now, be off! And try to make better use of your time.'

"Trusting in their leader's promises, the dragons obeyed, flying into the sky like fluttering ribbons. They gazed down at the parched earth and the pathetic people and waited eagerly for the rain to come."

"Let me guess," Hay Lin whispered with a sigh. "No rain?"

Her mother nodded somberly and went on with the story.

"Ten days passed after the emperor's promise," she said, "and they were ten days without any rain. The women had nothing with which to nourish their children. Some people ate tree bark. Some ate roots. And some . . ."

As her mother continued to tell the tragic

tale, the images in Hay Lin's head began to change. Instead of a scaly creature as big as a freight train, she pictured one of her classmates at the Sheffield Institute, wearing a long cape topped by a cardboard dragon's head. She imagined the tall boy in her algebra class with a cotton-floss beard glued to his smooth chin. He was smirking arrogantly, just like the emperor in the story.

Hay Lin's fantasies had begun to take shape in her mind—as a play! The play Mrs. Knickerbocker had assigned her to write and direct.

Hey, she thought excitedly, I was beginning to think old Mrs. Knickerbocker was crazy for giving me this assignment. But maybe, just maybe, I have what it takes to create the perfect play.

The key, of course, was to cast the central figures—the four dragons—perfectly. And Hay Lin knew just who would fit in each role. That was, of course, if all the actors wanted the parts!

The earth-loving yellow dragon was pure Cornelia. After all, Cornelia's prettiest feature was her long curtain of fine, blond hair. And as the Guardian with power over the earth, she could make vines grow or cause cracks in the ground with a simple flick of her finger—a motion that effortlessly tossed forth waves of green-tinted magic.

The pearl dragon was shy and quiet but for the powerful gusts of smoke and fire that it often sent pouring from its lungs.

That's totally Taranee, Hay Lin thought with a grin. She may be able to blow things up with her mind or conjure candle flames to light our way, but inside, she's the most even-keeled of any of us!

And the red dragon, the grandest of the four?

Irma, Hay Lin thought with a nod of satisfaction. Irma is nothing if not the center of attention. She's got a joke for every occasion, she's a total flirt, and our teachers are always giving her demerits for whispering in class. Irma's irrepressible. Plus, she controls water, and the red dragon wants to help put an end to the drought, with the help of the others.

And what about the slender black dragon, who darted through the air with the ease of a hummingbird?

I guess that would be me! Hay Lin thought. She fiddled with one of her glossy, blue-black pigtails and smiled. After all, I am the smallest girl in our group and in control of air. I am the only one who can fly—our group's own frequent flier.

But what about Will? Hay Lin wondered with a frown. Where does she fit into this picture?

It was a good question.

Of all five Guardians of the Veil, Will had the role that was the most mysterious. Hers was the power that linked her four pals to the Heart of Candracar. The Heart of Candracar was a glass orb encased in a beautiful, silver clasp. Stored deep within Will's being, it emerged from her palm whenever the Guardians—or the earthlings they were charged with protecting—were in need of its strength.

Holding all that power in the palm of her hand, Will was slightly different from the other Guardians. That power made her their leader—a reluctant leader at times, but a leader nonetheless.

Since learning about their magical destinies, Will had had to deal with some doubts from the other Guardians about her ability to be a good leader. But Will continued to prove that she was a great leader.

That's not surprising, Hay Lin thought with a grim nod. Will is basically our general in a war—a war with Prince Phobos! He was the evil ruler of Meridian, and intent on destroying the Veil.

Once upon a time, earth and Metamoor had coexisted peacefully. Then, an evil prince—Phobos—had come into power. He had ruled Metamoor ruthlessly. In fact, he had conquered it, absorbing its light, its happiness, its very life force into his own body. With all that energy, he had created a beautiful fortress for himself. He had stayed in that wondrous palace, locked away from his people, and oblivious to their suffering.

But that hadn't been enough for the greedy Phobos. Soon, he had set his sights on earth as well, wanting to feed on the planet's beauty and its goodness and undoubtedly to destroy it in the process.

That was when the Oracle of Candracar had stepped in.

Candracar was a place somewhere between

space and infinity, where benevolent beings lived who watched over the earth and sought to protect its people. The leader of these beings was the Oracle—an all-knowing and infinitely kind creature. He was the one who had created the Veil between earth and Metamoor.

For centuries, that barrier had stood between the worlds, keeping earth safe from the green, scaly reptiles and the thuggish, blue creatures who had wanted to cross over from Metamoor. All had been well—until the millennium hit. Great cosmic forces had damaged the Veil, making it weak. Holes had formed in twelve spots in the barrier, and those holes had become portals—tunnels that were a direct route between Metamoor and earth. As it happened, all of the portals had opened in Hay Lin's very own hometown of Heatherfield.

And that was why Hay Lin and her friends had been perfect choices for Guardians of the Veil. Using Hay Lin's grandmother as a messenger, the Oracle had anointed each of the girls with that title and bestowed upon them their magical powers.

And ever since, it had been drama, drama, drama. The girls had fought against Prince

Phobos's slimy henchman, Cedric. They'd watched their sweet, wan friend Elyon discover that she was Phobos's long-lost sister and defect to Metamoor's dark palace. And then they'd endured Elyon's taunts and torments as she had tried to get the Guardians to cross over to the dark side with her.

Recently, things had begun to change. The Guardians had seen Elyon begin to doubt her brother's intentions. She'd even considered joining forces with Metamoor's rebels, who wanted to free the people from poverty and hardship.

But, Hay Lin thought as she continued to listen to her mother's story with one ear, it's not clear yet in which direction Elyon will turn. Has she really decided not to go the evil route? Or is she deceiving us yet again?

Hay Lin yawned and snuggled deeper under the covers as the end of her mother's story drew near.

I'll come up with a part for Will tomorrow, Hay Lin thought as her eyes fluttered closed. For now, I'll think about the minor characters. I think Harry Dakin would make a perfect shrub. And what about Lenny Kalinsky? What should he be? Maybe the tree?

As Hay Lin tried to picture Lenny in her play, her mother finished her story and clicked off the light on the cluttered nightstand.

Then her mother tiptoed out of the room.

Hay Lin let herself fall into a deep sleep. The last image in her mind before she drifted off was Lenny Kalinsky, dressed up as a short tree.

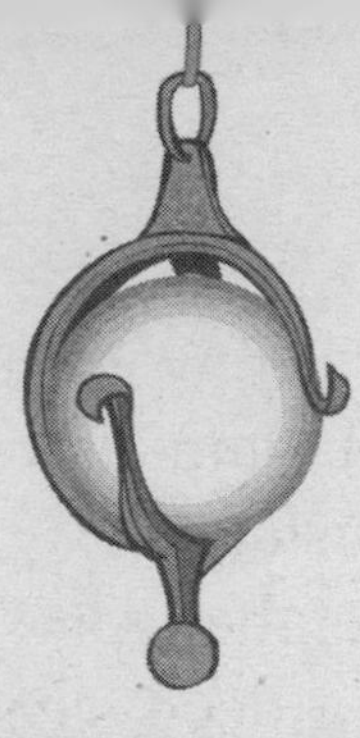

TWO

Lenny Kalinsky was dressed up as a leafy oak tree. Taranee gazed at him as he stood in the middle of the stage of Sheffield's auditorium. Lenny totally looked the part. His tanned face, complete with a bird's nest–like thatch of thick, brown hair, poked out of a brown felt trunk, sewn that very morning by Hay Lin. Lenny was picture-perfect, except for one thing . . . the fact that trees can't talk, Taranee thought, with a little giggle.

"Hey," Lenny said to a boy onstage, who was crouching at his feet and awkwardly grabbing at the bottom of his tree costume, "let go of my roots!"

Leaning against the auditorium wall next to Taranee were Will and Cornelia. They all were working hard to stifle their laughter as they watched Hay Lin *attempt* to turn Lenny into a strong, silent tree.

"Stop!" Hay Lin cried. She was standing at the base of the stage, clutching a thick script in her fist. Shaking her head so hard her pigtails made a distinct swishing sound, she hopped up onto the stage.

"What is it this time?" she demanded of Lenny.

Lenny pointed an arm—well, a branch—at the disgruntled Sheffielder at his feet.

"If he lifts up my roots," Lenny complained, "you'll be able to see my shoes."

"This is just a rehearsal, Lenny," Hay Lin sighed. "Forget about your shoes. Nobody will even notice them."

"No one will notice any of me!" Lenny blustered angrily. "Because this part is way too small! I don't want to be a tree."

"Fine," Hay Lin yelled. Her green plaid skirt swirled around her knees as she twisted to point out into the auditorium. The big room was thronged with Sheffielders clutching various dragon masks and bamboo-handled fans. They were all waiting to audition for the remaining parts in Hay Lin's play.

"*Don't* be the tree," Hay Lin challenged Lenny. "There are plenty of people out there who'd be willing to take your place."

A portly boy wearing a halo of green branches around his middle started to step up onto the stage.

"Like me, you mean!" he chirped. "I'll be a tree, Hay Lin!"

"Not you, Harry," Hay Lin scowled. "You're already playing the shrub!"

At that comment, Taranee couldn't hold her laughter in any longer. She nudged Will as she giggled. The two Guardians exchanged identical, amused looks as Cornelia said, "Well, looks like our little Hay Lin is really showing her true colors!"

"Hey," Will agreed, still smiling, "it's tough making everybody get along in a school play."

Taranee knew that Will was probably feeling the exact same way she was. They were very proud of their totally artsy friend, Hay Lin. But Taranee was also glad that *she* didn't have to negotiate with trees, shrubs, and dozens of other players in this Asian extravaganza.

Recognizing similar thoughts behind Will's

brown eyes, Taranee felt a wave of warmth wash over her. She and Will really did speak the same language.

It had been that way ever since their first days at Sheffield Institute. They had both just moved to Heatherfield and been newbies at the school. In fact, they'd met because both of them had gotten lost on their way to class. In the following days of navigating the school's foreign grounds, of desperately seeking lunch partners, of scoping out new crushes, the two sorta shy, new kids had totally bonded.

And of course, Taranee thought, once we found out we were both Guardians of the Veil, the deal was sealed. Will and I are definitely best friends.

At least, Taranee hoped they were.

After all, a lot had changed since Will and Taranee had first met. Will had become the group's leader, and an increasingly self-assured one at that. In the back of her mind, Taranee worried a little that Will would end up getting impatient with Taranee's more quiet and laid-back nature.

Then again, Taranee wasn't quite as quiet as she had used to be. Once upon a time, she'd been pretty shy and totally bookish.

Now, Taranee mused wryly, I've acquired a new hobby—throwing fireballs! And thinking about Nigel.

Behind her big, round glasses, Taranee cast her eyes down and blushed. She couldn't help it. Nigel was *so* cute. She still couldn't quite believe how much she liked him!

In fact, Taranee thought, as she gazed across the auditorium at Hay Lin bickering with Lenny, life is pretty sweet at the moment. I've got a whole quartet of best friends, a crush, *and* magical powers. Now, if only I didn't have to worry about saving the world, I'd be golden!

Taranee laughed again. Only a short time ago, she'd been totally freaked by the Guardian role.

I guess spending a few weeks in a Metamoorian prison snapped me out of *that*, Taranee thought. With a shiver, she thought back on the ghastly experience.

It had all been Elyon's doing. She'd tried to lure the Guardians over to her side. When they'd refused, she'd arranged to have Taranee kidnapped, locking her in a stark turret in Phobos's castle. As if that weren't enough,

Elyon had also tried to convince Taranee that Will and the others had abandoned her.

Her friends had ended up coming to her rescue. But Taranee had been surprised when it was her own strength and anger, not the actions of the other Guardians, that had helped her break through her glass cage and become free.

Ever since then, Taranee had been walking just a little taller in the hallways of the Sheffield Institute.

Yup, Taranee thought happily. Only a truly serious troublemaker could mess with me now!

"Hmmm, looks like trouble," said a low, gurgly voice at Taranee's left.

Taranee glanced over to see two girls peeking into the auditorium. One was tall and skinny, the other short and squat. But they both had the same straight, black hair, styled in practical, bowl cuts, the same small eyes, darting foxlike around the room, and the same notepads and pens.

They grinned at the stage, where Lenny was declaring to Hay Lin, "The truth is, your story's just plain silly."

"Oooh," said the shorter of the girls next to Taranee. Her voice was high and gratingly shrill. "Trouble is definitely brewing in the rehearsal hall," she squeaked.

The pair slithered into the auditorium and began skulking among the students who were waiting to audition. They paused before a girl gazing longingly at a red dragon mask. A half hour earlier, Hay Lin had told the girl she was too little for the part. And now, the girl was airing her anger to the meddlesome newcomers. Taranee couldn't help noticing the pair.

Will had noticed, too.

"Who are those two?" Taranee asked Cornelia. Cornelia was an Infielder (which was code for *popular kid*) at their school, and had been ever since kindergarten. If you wanted any of the Sheffield scoop, Cornelia was the girl to go to.

"Those are the Grumper sisters," Cornelia told Will and Taranee with a sniff. "Courtney and Bess. They write the gossip column for the school paper. And they're two really crabby, nasty girls."

Suddenly, a familiar voice rang out next to the trio.

"Two nasty witches is more like it!"

Taranee smiled as she turned to the voice. It

was Irma. She was scowling at a bulletin board on the auditorium wall.

"The Grumpers' names are on the list for Friday's tryouts," Irma complained.

Will, Cornelia, and Taranee walked over to where she stood.

"Well, don't forget," Will said, "your name's up there, too!"

"Way to go, Irma," Cornelia said slyly. "That means your dates—er, excuse me, your *tutoring sessions*—with Martin must really be working."

Irma pushed out her lower lip as her cheeks reddened. Taranee could see her working herself up to a snappy comeback.

Because Irma's *never* without one of those, Taranee thought admiringly. She definitely puts the *wit* in W.i.t.c.h.

But this time, Hay Lin beat Irma to the punch. She had just stomped into her friends' midst. Now she was gritting her teeth and declaring, "That Lenny is such a creep. My story is *not* silly!"

"Calm down, Hay Lin," Taranee declared with a grin. "All great artists are destined to be misunderstood!"

Taranee thought she saw a smile start to tug at the corners of Hay Lin's tight mouth. But then, the grumbly voice of Bess Grumper invaded the Guardians' space, putting a stop to Taranee's effort to cheer her friend up. Hay Lin's frown deepened. She looked down and kicked irritably at the edge of a tile in the floor. Bess smiled snidely at the girls.

"Well, look who we have here," she said. "The inseparable five."

To Taranee's surprise, she found herself the focus of Bess's sister Courtney's attention.

"You must be Taranee," Bess said, her voice dripping with false sweetness. "But you don't seem at all like the weirdo Cornelia says you are!"

Taranee gasped. She felt as though she'd been punched in the stomach. When Taranee had first met Cornelia, she'd been totally intimidated. Cornelia was tall, beautiful, effortlessly popular, and endlessly hip—not at all like the shy Taranee.

Nevertheless, Cornelia had always been welcoming toward Taranee. It hadn't taken long before Taranee had felt a true friendship blossoming between them.

Except, Taranee thought in despair, it seems that wasn't true. It must all have been an act. Cornelia was just pretending to like me because I was a fellow Guardian. She was just tolerating me because she *had* to.

Taranee whirled around to face Cornelia, one of her beaded braids slapping her cheek with a *thwack*. She barely noticed. She was too intent on glaring at Cornelia, whose pretty blue eyes had gone wide with surprise.

"So, you think I'm a weirdo, huh?" Taranee asked accusingly.

"What on earth are you talking about?" Cornelia asked, looking from Taranee to the Grumper sisters in confusion. She had been talking to Irma and Will and not heard the Grumpers' comment.

The Grumpers shrugged, smiled, and turned their backs on the pair. Now, they smiled obnoxiously at the glowering Irma and the brooding Hay Lin.

"You look worried, Irma," Courtney simpered. "Are you afraid you won't do well in your audition? Or are you just scared of the costumes Hay Lin's going to design for you to wear in the play?"

"Huh?" Hay Lin peeped. More hurt flashed in her dark eyes.

That was when Courtney moved in for the kill.

"Oh, don't get upset," she said, darting over to Hay Lin to drape an arm over her shoulders. "I'm sure Irma was just exaggerating when she said you had horrible taste!"

"What?" Hay Lin barked, twisting herself away from Courtney's grasp to glare at her bud. "Irma!"

"That's not true," Irma protested. "I never said anything like that."

Hay Lin growled skeptically. Things were getting way too tense. Taranee almost wanted to see what Irma would say next. But she was too angry at Cornelia to pay any more attention to Hay Lin's verbal duel with Irma. She had to get back to her own battle!

"Cornelia!" she said. "I thought you were my friend!"

"B—but, but . . ." Cornelia protested.

"Take it back!" Taranee yelled in a hurt voice, "or . . . or . . ."

Taranee stopped herself before she voiced the threat that was forming in her mind. A threat that consisted of balls of fire, hurled from her magical hands toward her enemies. Taranee could already feel her fingertips tingling with budding swirls of hot, orange magic.

"Don't be ridiculous!" Cornelia snapped, looking pointedly at Taranee's fluttering fingers.

Taranee took a deep breath, then clenched her fists, containing her magical impulse.

Cornelia was right, Taranee admitted to herself. If she had unleashed her powers in public, the Guardians would have been exposed. And they'd most definitely have been singled out as total freaks!

Oh, and Cornelia would *hate* that, Taranee thought, feeling another surge of anger in her belly. We can't have little Miss Popular standing out in a crowd, can we? Any more than we can have her hanging out with a *weirdo*!

Her anger renewed, Taranee growled, "I said, take it back, Cornelia!"

"You're not going to believe those two troublemakers, are you?" Cornelia snapped.

Before Taranee could reply, the troublemakers themselves spoke up.

"It's getting late!" Courtney chirped with a smug little smile. "We'd better get going!"

"Yeah, you'd better," Will added, glaring at the Grumpers.

Taranee was glad to see Will stand up to the Grumpers. But that still didn't make her forget Cornelia's slight.

Those sisters may be annoying, she thought irritably, but Cornelia's the one who called me a weirdo.

Taranee was about to hurl that very thought at Cornelia when Will stepped between the feuding friends with an announcement.

"Hey, Taranee," she said. "Your brother's here."

"Huh?" Taranee said. Reluctantly, she tore her gaze away from Cornelia and glanced at the auditorium door. Slouching against it was, indeed, her older brother, Peter. His long dreadlocks were scooped up into a ponytail on the top of his head. In his stylishly fingerless-gloved hands was a crumpled brown paper bag and a familiar-looking green textbook.

"Peter!" Taranee said. When she saw her brother, some of her tension melted away. Not only was Peter totally protective, in the way all big brothers should be, but he also exuded a cool, breezy, surfer-boy vibe. His ease among people was infectious—and comforting.

"What are you doing here?" Taranee asked happily as she stumbled over to him—and turned her back on Cornelia.

"Just being your delivery boy," Peter drawled. "You forgot some things when you left the house this morning."

"My lunch and my homework!" Taranee blurted out, shaking her head at her own absentmindedness. "Thanks, big brother!"

"No prob," Peter said with a shrug and a glittery smile.

That was when Taranee *really* started to feel better. Peter always came to her rescue. And on this occasion, he definitely made her feel special, because he had made a trip to Sheffield, just for her.

Or *had* it been just for her? At that moment, Peter's laughing brown eyes were skimming right over Taranee to land on Cornelia!

"Hi, Cornelia!" he called out, giving Taranee's slender cohort his most charming grin. Then he loped out of the auditorium.

As Peter's pom-pom of dreads disappeared behind the swinging auditorium doors, Cornelia waved good-bye. Then she cast her big eyes down, as a flush spread across her pale cheeks.

Ex-*cuse* me? Taranee sputtered to herself. Not only is Cornelia dissing me, now she's flirting with my brother?

Oh, boy, Taranee thought, glowering at Cornelia's pretty face. This is going to get ugly!

THREE

Cornelia watched as Peter sauntered toward the auditorium doors. She found herself mesmerized by his long, lanky strides, the casual turn of his head, and the confident warmth of his smile. When she finally lifted her hand to return the cute guy's friendly wave, Cornelia realized she was too late. Peter had already strolled through the doors, his dreadlocks bouncing casually out of view.

He was gone.

But Cornelia felt as if he were still there, radiating charisma. A wave of heat was rushing to her face, reddening her cheeks. She felt her heart pounding. A shy smile was forcing itself onto her face—a smile that should not have been there. After all, only an instant earlier,

Cornelia had been locked in a standoff with Taranee. And she'd been totally enraged at those silly, lying Grumpers.

Now, the only thing Cornelia was thinking about was her new crush. Wait! I like—like Peter Cook?

B—but how can I like Peter, Cornelia thought, when I'm in love with Caleb?

The very thought of Caleb made Cornelia feel a stab of pain and yearning.

She'd first seen Caleb in a dream. In one of her daydreams, she'd imagined the perfect boy. He had big, sad, green eyes and silky, brown hair. He wore a long, brown coat and chunky, black boots. It was a warrior's wardrobe—as strong as his boyish face was sweet. There was kindness in his eyes, and he had the sweetest smile.

After that first dream, Cornelia had seen the mystery boy again and again. She'd find herself drawing him in the margins of her notebooks or spotting him in a Heatherfield crowd. Back when Elyon had been Cornelia's best friend, she had even drawn a portrait of the boy for Cornelia. It had been a perfect rendering and a treasured gift from her friend.

But the guy had been only a fantasy—or so Cornelia had thought. Then, she'd taken a trip to Metamoor. Dark and Gothic, inhabited by scaly, green lizards and monstrous, cobalt-colored thugs, Metamoor had positively oozed gloom and doom. It had been the last place Cornelia would have expected to discover her dream boy.

He had actually found her. Cornelia had traveled to Metamoor by way of a portal, one that had emerged in a fountain in a bustling village square. The fountain had turned out to be mega-deep—too deep for Cornelia to make it back to the surface.

Had the five Guardians made the trip together, Irma would have conjured up a bubble of air from the water to give Cornelia a breather. Or Will would have summoned the power of the Heart of Candracar to save her from drowning.

But Cornelia had kept her friends out of the loop and gone alone on the trip. She'd been the only one who'd wanted to track Elyon down and prove that her best friend had not become completely evil.

So Cornelia had been trapped all alone in

the murky deep of the fountain portal. She'd almost drowned.

Caleb, her dream boy, had saved her. He'd reached into the fountain and fished her out. When Cornelia had blinked the water out of her eyes, she'd been stunned to find that Caleb was the boy she'd been dreaming about for as long as she could remember. Only this time he was real.

Miraculously, she was not the only one to have dreamed of the meeting. Caleb had seen Cornelia in his dreams as well.

So, it was going to be a happy ending, right? Cornelia had thought. We go on a date, become boyfriend and girlfriend, and go to the prom. End of story.

Well, not quite.

The problem with Caleb was, he wasn't exactly human, even if he did look like a total rock 'n' roll hottie. He was the leader of Metamoor's rebels. With a band of scruffy soldiers, he was fighting to free that world's people from Phobos's oppression. He was also trying to help Elyon claim her destiny as a kind and good ruler of Metamoor.

All that rebel work didn't leave much time

for splitting milkshakes, hitting the mall, or romantic strolls.

What it all boils down to, Cornelia thought now, with a sigh, is that Caleb and I are both on life-or-death missions. We're each trying to save our own worlds. We're as far apart as any two beings can possibly be.

In fact, she went on, feeling a sharp pang in her chest, I may never see him again! I'll have only the magical, white flower he gave me to remember him by. A flower he made out of one of my tears.

On the other hand, it was hard to imagine sunny, laid-back Peter ever making her cry, Cornelia thought. Peter was as sweet and normal as a slice of cherry pie or a sunny day at the beach or—

Or the way my life used to be, Cornelia thought sadly, before I became a Guardian. I wonder what life would be like if I'd never become magical; if I'd never had my heart broken when I was torn away from Caleb only minutes after we'd met. Maybe I *would* be Peter's girlfriend now. Maybe we'd go on ordinary movie dates together. I could help him study for his exams and he could teach me how to surf. We'd be happy together. Simply happy. Or would we?

"Oooh, check it out!"

Cornelia was jolted from her daydream by the harsh and squeaky voice of Courtney Grumper. Hadn't she and that busybody Bess left yet?

"The prom queen is totally blushing," Courtney said to her sister in a very loud stage whisper.

"Well, that guy *was* cute," Bess replied. "Don't you think?"

Wait a minute, Cornelia thought in alarm. Did Bess Grumper just declare Peter—*my* Peter—cute?

"What are you saying?" Cornelia demanded, stalking over to Bess.

"I just said he was cute," Bess said with a smug smile. "And I bet he thinks *you*'re cute, too."

"You—you really think so?" Cornelia gasped, giggling in surprise and embarrassment. Bess hadn't been moving in on her turf at all. She must have finally started using her gossipy ways for good! "Bess, how do you know that? What have you heard?"

"It's no secret!" Bess said. "You two would make a cute couple."

Cornelia had only an instant to grow giddy before she saw Bess's plain face cloud over.

"It's too bad," Bess lamented.

"What's too bad?" Cornelia asked breathlessly.

"Your friend Will," Courtney shrugged, looking at Bess, who nodded in confirmation. "*She* seems to think Peter's cute, too."

"That probably explains," Bess said breezily, "why she told Peter you'd never go out with him."

"Will told him that?" Cornelia gasped in shock.

"Like the saying goes," Courtney simpered, "'Incredible but true!' If I hadn't heard it with my own ears, I wouldn't believe it, either. And I certainly wouldn't be telling you."

Cornelia felt her heart pounding in her chest once again, but the feeling was decidedly *un*-dreamy this time. She turned away from the Grumpers to face Will, who hadn't been paying any attention to the exchange. She had been too busy gazing worriedly at Hay Lin and Irma, who were snarling at each other.

"Thanks a lot, Will," Cornelia snapped. "Really!"

Will jumped at the sound of her name, then gazed at Cornelia with wide, innocent eyes.

"Cornelia, what are you talking about?" Will asked.

"Why do you have to stick your nose into other people's business?" Cornelia demanded.

"What are you talking about?" Will asked again.

"About Peter!" Cornelia sniffed. She planted her fists on her narrow hips. "Why did you have to go around telling people I don't like him?"

"I—I didn't—"

"Uh-huh," Cornelia interrupted. "Well, let me tell *you* something, little Will . . ."

As Cornelia began to unleash her frustration upon her friend, the increasingly bewildered look on Will's face didn't calm her. It only enraged her more.

Elyon, Cornelia thought as she bawled Will out, would never have betrayed me like this. She was the only true friend I had. Now, she's gone!

And, it appeared, so were the Grumper sisters—slithering out of the auditorium with smug smiles on their faces. If Cornelia had been a little less angry, she might have noticed their departure.

Of course, if she'd been a little less angry, she might not have believed those troublemakers in the first place.

But the sad fact was that Cornelia *was* that angry. And telling Will off for a full five minutes did nothing to make her feel any better. So she simply stomped out of the auditorium and flounced into one of Sheffield's hallways that opened onto the courtyard, for a breath of fresh air. As she gazed through one of the passage's dramatic archways, Cornelia was vaguely aware of the other Guardians rushing out behind her.

She stiffened, waiting for Will to touch her shoulder and apologize for her actions.

Or for Hay Lin and Irma to fall, giggling, into each other's arms, having made up instantly, the way they always did.

She even thought Taranee might have sidled up to her side, apologizing for her harsh accusations.

But none of those things happened. All five

girls remained glumly silent, each taking up stations in a different part of the hall. Hay Lin pulled out some school papers, making a lame attempt to study them. But the rest of the girls simply stared into the distance—scowling and sulking.

The Power of Five? Cornelia thought angrily. What a joke!

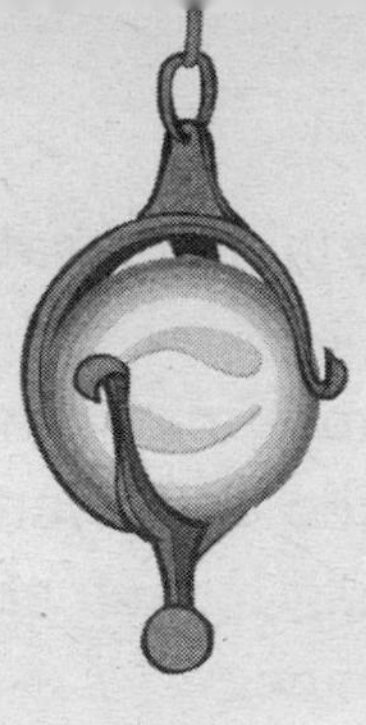

FOUR

Will slumped against the banister and marveled at the horrible mood that had overtaken her friends. Only a few yards away, a crowd of Sheffielders were squealing and giggling in a snowball fight. But up here, the vibe was positively gloomy.

Hay Lin bit her lip to keep from crying as she shuffled through her papers.

Cornelia stood with her back turned and her arms crossed in front of her.

Taranee hid her face behind the fuzzy earflaps of her winter hat.

And Irma was pursing her glossy lips in a petulant pout.

Just great, Will thought. If Cedric showed up right now, he'd have us beat in an instant.

Though Cedric was a long-haired babe when he was in his human form, he could transform himself on a whim into a mammoth snake. Each time he'd attacked the Guardians, it had taken every ounce of magic, strength, *and* camaraderie they had to escape.

Will blew a lock of red hair out of her eyes and glared at her friends. *Especially* Cornelia. She couldn't believe that cool, worldly Cornelia had bought the Grumpers' silly story about her liking Peter.

Actually, she couldn't believe any of this stuff was going down between any of them!

She gazed sullenly at her friends.

"Come on, guys," she declared seriously. "Who wants to start?"

"Start what?" Taranee asked gloomily.

"Talking!" Will sputtered. "Do you really want to stand around here sulking all day?"

Apparently, Cornelia did.

"I have nothing to say to you," she said, turning away as she adjusted her pink headband.

That's no surprise, Will thought irritably. Could Cornelia be any more stubborn?

Once upon a time, Will might have considered Cornelia's aloofness intimidating. But, after months of leading the Guardians, Will had learned to trust herself and speak her mind. And that was what she was going to do right now.

"Well," she said, "I *do* have something to say. I don't know the Grumper sisters, but it's pretty clear to me that they get a kick out of making people fight."

Cornelia tossed her long, silky hair and sniffed. Taranee looked—if possible—even sadder than she had a moment before. Irma just shrugged. Hay Lin flipped through her papers faster.

"Don't you think," Will demanded, "we have more reasons to get along than we have to fight?"

Will couldn't believe it. Her friends were *still* sulking! She pressed on.

"Together, we've faced terrible things," she reminded her friends. "The lies of two bigmouths shouldn't separate us!"

Finally, Hay Lin made a move toward Will.

"Will's right," she said to the others. She looked shyly down at her sheaf of papers.

That's Hay Lin's play script, Will suddenly

realized. She's been studying it endlessly for days, now.

"I wanted the end of the play to be a surprise," Hay Lin said quietly, "but maybe the time has come for you guys to know the whole story of the four dragons."

"That does sound good," Irma said, making Will smile slightly. Irma could never stay mad at Hay Lin for long.

"But why now?" Irma asked.

"Just listen, and you'll understand," Hay Lin assured the girls, who'd clustered around her at the edge of the breezeway. "I couldn't believe it myself when my mom told me."

Will felt a little surge of excitement shoot through her chest.

"Okay, Hay Lin," she declared. "I'm curious! At the rehearsal, you left off at the part about the people going hungry."

"Right," Hay Lin said. She glanced back at her script, and began to speak. As she did, her face took on a distant, glowing quality. Despite the goofy goggles planted on top of her head and her puffy winter coat, Hay Lin looked positively ethereal.

Just the way an air goddess should, Will

thought, with another smile. Will was glad to feel her anger ebbing away.

"The four dragons," Hay Lin began, "decided to help the starving people. And it was the red dragon who figured out how."

As Hay Lin described the scene in her play, the images in Will's mind began to morph. She no longer saw Lenny Kalinsky in a homespun tree costume, or even standing on the small stage of the Sheffield auditorium.

Suddenly, Will imagined she was flying through crystalline, blue skies with four majestic dragons. Their scales were beautiful—iridescent red, yellow, black, and white. Their faces, despite their pointy horns, flared nostrils, and beady, yellow eyes, were kind and wise.

Will listened as Hay Lin continued to narrate her tale: "'The sea!' the red dragon declared to his comrades as they slithered in the air around him. 'All the water we could want is there. And with that water, we could help those people. We just have to scoop it up in our mouths and spray it into the sky over their fields. It will turn into rain and fall onto the crops.'

"And that's what the four dragons did,

hundreds and hundreds of times," Hay Lin went on. "The people couldn't believe their eyes."

As Hay Lin told the tale, Will felt herself become part of the story, almost as if she were there. Will pictured a poor villager with hungry eyes and a nearly empty bowl of gruel. The woman was slumped against a rock, too weak to even drag herself inside, to a table. The woman was spooning the thin porridge into her mouth in small, measured bites, trying to stretch out the grim meal.

Plink.

Out of nowhere, a droplet of water fell smack-dab into the skinny woman's breakfast.

The woman looked up in shock and confusion.

Plink!

Another raindrop! This time, it hit the woman's pale cheek.

Plinkplinkplink . . . whoooooosh!

The isolated drops became a full-scale rain shower! The parched earth began to soak the moisture up greedily as the villagers streamed out of their homes, gaping at the wet sky in shock, wonder, and finally, joy.

"Rain! *Rain!*" they cried. They let the drops fall onto their tongues, soak their dusty hair, and spatter their dirty clothes.

"They were saved!" Hay Lin exclaimed to her friends, her cheeks growing pink, as she became caught up in the moment.

Hay Lin's excitement brought Will back to the present. She listened as Hay Lin continued: "They were happier than they'd been in generations. But the Jade Emperor was *not* pleased with the dragons' deed. He was outraged.

"'Arrest them!' he ordered his people, 'and bring them here immediately.'

"The dragons were taken to the palace in chains," Hay Lin continued, somber once again. "The emperor had prepared a terrible punishment for them."

"Worse than having to listen to the story of the four dragons?" Irma asked with an exaggerated yawn. But then she winked at Hay Lin and nodded eagerly. She was only kidding. She wanted to hear the rest of the tale just as much as the rest of the group did.

"It took a hundred men to hold each dragon down," Hay Lin said.

Again, Will pictured the scene: a grand

palace on a cliff, overlooking the sea that the emperor guarded. A walled courtyard, big enough to contain four massive dragons, manacled around their snouts and powerful limbs.

Hay Lin continued. "'You have challenged my power,' the emperor roared at the dragons, 'and for that, you will be punished. Here is my order to the mountain spirit, who *will* obey me: Lock these dragons up in four separate mountains. Make sure they will never be able to leave.'

"The red dragon was brave enough to protest," Hay Lin said. "'But we only did what was right,' he said.

"The emperor had no pity for the dragons. His order was carried out."

Now Will pictured a flat landscape just beyond the emperor's sprawling palace. Looking out at the enormous meadow, a black-robed mystic threw his arms into the air. He muttered magical incantations and summoned up the mountain spirit, who created four unforgiving, if beautiful, prisons: four mountains.

Each dragon was absorbed into one of the mountains, much as the glowing Heart of Candracar had been absorbed into Will's palm.

But unlike Will's amulet—which often freed itself from her body to activate the Guardians' magical powers—the dragons remained locked away, with no way to escape or be released.

"Your wish has been granted, Your Majesty," Will could hear the weary mystic saying to the evil ruler.

"That is what happens to those who rouse my anger," the emperor would have growled toward the four mountains. "Now, they will never be able to interfere again!"

It was only a fairy tale, but the injustice of the emperor's decision angered Will. So, when Hay Lin's story took an unexpected—and hopeful—turn, she caught her breath.

"With a brilliant flash of light," Hay Lin narrated, "a beautiful woman suddenly appeared out of thin air before the emperor. Her long, blue-black hair was piled on top of her head in a noble chignon. Her skin was like fine porcelain. Her black eyes were piercing and intelligent. And her robes were made of purple silk, fluttering gracefully in a magical wind. She was completely cool!"

Will couldn't help giggling.

"Really?" she asked. "Is that how the

ancient tale goes? 'Completely cool?'"

"Hey, don't interrupt the playwright," Hay Lin admonished with a grin. "Don't you want to know who this woman was? She was the nymph Xin Jing, a woman of courage and great power, who was angered by the emperor's actions."

"Xin Jing?" Will breathed softly, loving the *shoosh*ing feel of the nymph's name on her tongue.

"It means *Heart of Crystal*," Hay Lin said, giving Will a pointed look.

Will frowned. This dragon tale was starting to sound awfully familiar.

"The nymph's words were severe," Hay Lin now read from her script, breaking into Will's thoughts. "'Your cruelty,' she scolded the emperor, 'is equaled only by your arrogance.'

"'And your beauty,' the emperor responded saucily, 'is unsurpassed, as always.'

"'You should look at the beauty of those mountains,' Xin Jing retorted, pointing toward the new peaks along the horizon. 'Look closely, because you will never see them like that again.'

"The nymph couldn't undo the emperor's

injustice," Hay Lin explained. "But she wanted the brave dragons' sacrifice to be remembered for eternity. So, she raised her arms into the air, unleashing great swirls of magic—rays of pink, green, orange, silver, and blue."

What? Will thought in disbelief and amazement. But those are the colors of *our* magic!

"The nymph rose into the air, her arms outstretched," Hay Lin continued.

Just like me, unleashing the power of the Heart of Candracar, Will thought, her eyes widening.

"She sent blasts of her power through the four mountains, releasing her magic into them," Hay Lin said seriously. "At the same time, she absorbed the dragon's essences from the mountains. Forever bound to the dragons, the nymph Xin Jing rose up over the world and turned the four dragons into four rivers: the black river, the yellow river, the red river, and the pearl river, the most important waterways in this Asian country."

"And the nymph," Will whispered, "Xin Jing. What happened to her?"

"All that was left to remember her by was a crystal amulet," Hay Lin said. She looked up from her script to address her friends with wide eyes. "This amulet contained the essence of the four dragons—and her own."

Will, Taranee, Cornelia, and Irma stared at Hay Lin in stunned silence, until Taranee broke the spell with an awed "Wow!"

"Those dragons and the nymph," Hay Lin said, voicing what they'd all realized by then, "—they're us, don't you see? That legend tells us the origins of our powers!"

"So," Will breathed, "the crystal amulet—"

"Yeah, Will," Hay Lin said with a nod. "It's the Heart of Candracar. This story was my grandma's favorite fairy tale. Now do you see why?"

Hay Lin turned now to Cornelia, whose long, blond hair spilled down her back like a golden waterfall.

"The yellow dragon loved the earth," Hay Lin said. She fingered her own black pigtails nervously. "And the black dragon flew better than the others.

"The red dragon loved the water, and the pearl dragon controlled fire," Hay Lin continued, pointing at Irma and Taranee.

"And the nymph," Will said, "all by herself,

made these transformations possible, right?"

Okay, so *first* I find out I'm magical, she thought incredulously. *Then* I learn that I have to lead the Guardians into battle to save the world. And *now*, to top it all off, I'm being told that I'm the descendant of an ancient, Asian nymph? Could my life get any freakier?

Or, a little voice in the back of Will's head piped up, more exciting? Either way, Will was beginning to think that she wanted to find out how it was all going to end. This was one story she definitely wanted to have a happy ending.

FIVE

We're descended from dragons? Irma thought in amazement. *Or is it rivers? Whatever it is, it's pretty cool.*

Irma grinned giddily. But a moment later, her smile faded.

Wait a minute, she realized. *I'm descended from a* scaly *dragon? Gross! And didn't Hay Lin also mention horns and a beard? Maybe this isn't as cool as I thought it was.*

Irma sighed grumpily.

"Hmmm," Cornelia said suddenly, glancing at her friends. "The story was a bit *long,* but poetic! No arguing that!"

Hay Lin giggled softly, and Taranee seemed to become a little less pale and trembly.

"What do you think of that story?" Taranee asked as the girls started walking through the breezeway for their first class. The school day was just about to start. "Dragons! Nymphs! Now that's what I call *real* magic."

"Oh?" Will said. "What does that mean? That, before, you thought our magic *wasn't* real?"

Taranee shrugged nodded sheepishly.

To tell the truth, Irma could see where Taranee was coming from. The girls had only been magical for a short time, but Irma was already totally used to it. Sometimes she forgot that not everybody had the ability to make waves in water with the wiggle of a finger. Or speak to the ocean. Or form a lifesaving air bubble around herself and her friends in the unlikely event that they had to make a landing on water.

It's a lot easier to accept being magical than to feud with my friends, Irma thought.

Impulsively, Irma nudged Hay Lin with her elbow.

"You know something, Hay Lin?" she said playfully, "your costumes aren't so bad, after all. Even though *I* never said they were."

"Thanks, Irma," Hay Lin said with a big grin and a roll of the eyes. Her expression silently said, *Who cares about those gossipy Grumpers?* We're *best friends, after all.*

As if she had read their minds, Cornelia said the words out loud: "Forget the Grumpers. My mom always says rumors need a sharp tongue—"

"—But they also need a willing ear," Taranee said with a laugh. "My mom says that, too."

Cornelia and Taranee exchanged their own secret, forgiving glance.

Will smiled, too.

"Okay, I get it," she declared. She stopped walking. Irma and the others stopped, too, looking at her quizzically.

"Guys," she said, "we've always got to be honest with each other, and if there's a problem, we've got to resolve it right away! Do we all promise?"

There was a time when Irma might have rolled her blue eyes at Will for going all Mom-like on them. But, after all they'd been through together, Irma wasn't just tolerant of Will's earnest leadership, she was grateful for it.

Well there's *another* surprise, Irma thought, shaking her head in wonder. Who knew I was such a team player?

She shrugged happily. And when the group yelled, "We promise!" Irma's voice was the loudest.

Irma bounced along happily as the girls resumed their stroll. Together, they descended a staircase that went from the breezeway to the snow-covered front lawn, then headed toward Sheffield's main building for their next class.

Irma was so glad the spat between her friends hadn't lasted very long. As if she wanted to deal with any more drama!

Unless, of course, Irma thought suddenly, that drama involved revenge!

"Our little peace treaty," she piped up as the girls walked along, "doesn't mean that the Grumpers should get away with their little scheme. No one can tell us lies and think they'll walk away free and clear. Those two made us believe horrible things about each other."

"We'll deal with them when the time is right," Cornelia said, squinting thoughtfully.

Irma frowned. Delaying a Grumpers put-down? How very boring.

Irma was about to fashion a retort when Hay Lin added another unfun note to the conversation.

"For now," she said to Irma, "you'd better just concentrate on your French test!"

Mon dieu! Irma thought, slapping her forehead. I had almost managed to shove that annoying exam out of my head. I can't believe my day is going to begin with such torture. Even watching Lenny Kalinsky play a tree would be less painful. I would totally bail on it if not for—

"Do you want a part in my play or don't you?" Hay Lin said.

Yeah, Irma thought ruefully. If not for *that*.

She and Hay Lin walked up the steps into the main building. The rest of the girls were heading in a different direction.

"There's still a leading role open," Hay Lin reminded Irma. "In just a couple more days, you could have a star on your bedroom door."

"There's just one hurdle to hop first," Irma said with a groan. "The French exam!"

The French exam! Irma thought again, a few

minutes later. This time, her groan was more heartfelt—because she had arrived at her French class. Test time was just moments away.

Irma slid into her chair just as the bell rang. Immediately, Madame Gounod began walking up and down the aisles, tossing an exam onto each desk. Irma gnawed on a hangnail anxiously as the severe, skinny instructor glared at her students over her reading glasses.

"If you've studied, this shouldn't be too difficult," she said, in that prim, pinched way of hers that drove Irma crazy. "You have one hour, starting right now."

Irma scanned the exam's first questions with a deep sigh. Planting her chin on her fists, she thought: If only this were an oral quiz. Then I could use my powers to decide what questions would be asked!

Around the same time Irma had discovered that she could make her bathwater boogie through the air, she'd had a few bizarre experiences at school. One of the early incidents had occurred one morning in history class. Irma had been having an ordinary day—passing notes back and forth with Hay Lin and doodling her latest crush's name in the margin of her notebook—when all of a sudden Mr. Collins had announced a pop quiz.

No! Irma had wailed inside her head. *It's so unfair of Mr. Collins to spring a quiz on us on a Wednesday morning. Boy Comet's on Tuesday nights. It's my fave show—and the perfect excuse to blow off studying.*

The only part she'd gotten to during the commercials was a little section on Mary, Queen of Scots.

Irma had crossed her fingers and whispered under her breath, "Please, ask about Mary, Queen of Scots. Please, Mr. Collins! Do it for Mary. Even if she did lose her head, she could still help me on this quiz."

As Irma muttered her wish, Mr. Collins had flipped through his textbook. He'd looked up and glanced straight at Irma, his mustache twitching mischievously.

"Ah, there's our class's biggest *Boy Comet* fan," he had said. "But I'm sure she also found time to study last night! Let's see. Irma? How, and on what date, did Mary, Queen of Scots lose her life?"

Irma had been almost too shocked to give her answer (which, by the way, was totally correct). Her wish for the right question had come true.

"What a coincidence," Irma had whispered to Hay Lin gleefully, telling her friend about her little prayer.

Several days and a few quizzes later, Irma was beginning to wonder what was going on. Her crossed fingers and fervent prayers were clearly rigging the oral quizzes. Every time she begged for a particular question, that's the one she received.

It had made it pretty easy for Irma to change her homework habits. Selective studying became her afternoon activity of choice, along with a lot more hanging with friends, experimenting with makeup and, oh, yeah, going on save-the-world missions to Metamoor.

The only subject that completely sabotaged Irma's slacker scheme?

French! Madame Gounod's quizzes were never oral. Gounod was all about *vrai* or *faux* (true or false) questions—and trick ones at that.

Irma bit her lip and attacked the first translation. To her surprise, the right answer came to her easily. She moved on to the next question.

That was a toughie—a conjugation Irma hadn't reviewed since the previous week.

But at least I recognize it! Irma thought. Smiling, she marked another *x*.

This test is different from those pop quizzes, she thought as she moved on to the next item. I can't cheat. And actually, I don't even want to cheat! True or false, right or wrong, magic has nothing to do with this test.

Irma leaned closer to her paper. She began crossing off letter after letter.

It's up to me and this sheet of paper, Irma thought, her pen moving with increasing confidence.

Irma gasped. Her name was *crossed out* on the tryout list for Hay Lin's play.

Talk about a way to kill a mood! Irma thought with a scowl. Here I've emerged from my French exam not five minutes ago, feeling totally triumphant. Then I happen to walk by the drama-club bulletin board on my way to biology, and I'm slapped in the face with this? I've been x-ed out of my shot at the lead role before I even had a chance to audition.

With a snarl, Irma turned her back on the

bulletin board. Her eyes widened. There was Hay Lin! She was walking down the hallway. When she saw Irma glowering next to the sign-up sheet, she grimaced. Clearly, she'd seen Irma's x-ed out name, too.

"Hey, Hay Lin!" Irma cried. She pointed over her shoulder at the sign-up sheet and demanded, "What's with the line through my name? Who kicked me out of the tryouts?"

"I had nothing to do with it, Irma," Hay Lin said morosely. "It was Ms. Kelly's decision."

The drama teacher? Irma thought. Cool, young, pretty Ms. Kelly? I can't believe it!

"She can't do this to me!" Irma squealed at Hay Lin. "I have a right to be in the play, too!"

Suddenly, a voice piped up behind Irma.

"Don't be mad at me!"

Irma turned to spot the traitor herself, Ms. Kelly, looking stunning in a pink turtleneck sweater. She also looked mega-guilty.

"Well, Ms. Kelly," Irma sputtered, "who should I be mad at, then?"

"I'm sorry," Ms. Kelly said, eyeing the sign-up sheet with a shrug. "But those are the rules. Until you've gotten your grade point average up, no school play."

"But, Ms. Kelly!" Irma protested. "Up until yesterday, I was on the list."

"Let's just say that that was an oversight," Ms. Kelly said with a sigh, running a hand through the shiny black ringlets piled atop her head. "And I would have been happy to continue overlooking it if the Grumper sisters hadn't pointed it out to the principal."

Irma felt her cheeks go hot with rage.

"Those two again!" she screeched. "I swear, this time I'm going to turn them into—into—"

Through the red haze that blurred her vision, Irma saw Hay Lin put a hand over her mouth, then glance in alarm at Ms. Kelly. Hay Lin could tell that Irma was on the verge of a magical moment—and a vengeful one!

She's right. I am out for revenge, Irma thought angrily. Wait till those Grumpers get a taste of my watery wrath.

She clenched her fists.

She focused on her inner Guardian.

But then, Irma did something curious—nothing. She didn't blow her top, and she *didn't* finish her threat.

This was a new development.

Not too long ago, Irma had made Martin

Tubbs become invisible at a party. She'd also turned a boy into a toad when he had gotten a little too fresh. That had only meant that she and her friends had had to hunt the warty guy down in an icky swamp so that she could undo the damage she had done.

After that, she'd learned to keep her magical powers—and her temper—under control.

But am I being rewarded for my total grown-upness? Irma thought indignantly. Not even. I take my French test without a lick of magical help, and I'm *still* shut out of the play.

"Is there anybody worse than the Grumper sisters?" Irma groaned aloud, slumping over in defeat.

"I really don't think so," Hay Lin sighed, patting Irma's shoulder.

That was when Will ambled up, slipping a notebook from her last class into her backpack. With one look at Irma's morose expression, her own face fell.

"Oh, no! Irma, did the test go badly?" she asked.

"I still don't know," Irma complained. "But everything else is going terribly! I can't go to tryouts until I find out my grade."

Irma hung her head. She felt dangerously close to bursting into tears!

Will came to the rescue.

"Cheer up, Irma," she said with a twinkle in her brown eyes. "We've definitely been through tougher situations. Don't think about it now. C'mon."

Will extended her arms to Irma, who couldn't resist the sweet gesture. She let Will give her a hug. And she even smiled.

Then, she burst out laughing—when something in Will's jacket began trembling and jumping, tickling Irma like mad.

"Wow, I only asked for a smile," Will giggled. "You don't need to start laughing at me."

Irma hopped away from her friend and kept giggling.

"I'm not laughing at you," she squealed. "Something in your jacket is shaking!"

Will glanced down in surprise.

"Oh!" she said. "It's my cell phone. I had it on VIBRATE."

"That buzzing sounds just like my dad's electric razor," Irma said as Will hit the cell's TALK button.

"Hello?" Will said. A moment later, her eyes

widened with surprise—and then grew even wider—with dread!

"Mrs. Rudolph?" Will said. "No, I can hear you. The connection's just a little fuzzy—"

Mrs. Rudolph! Irma thought with a heavy sigh. As if this day weren't enough of a bummer! A call from our math teacher, Mrs. Rudolph—otherwise known as a Metamoorian rebel—can only mean one thing. Trouble's brewing.

Which means I'm going to have to forget about French tests *and* annoying Grumpers—so we Guardians can do our jobs!

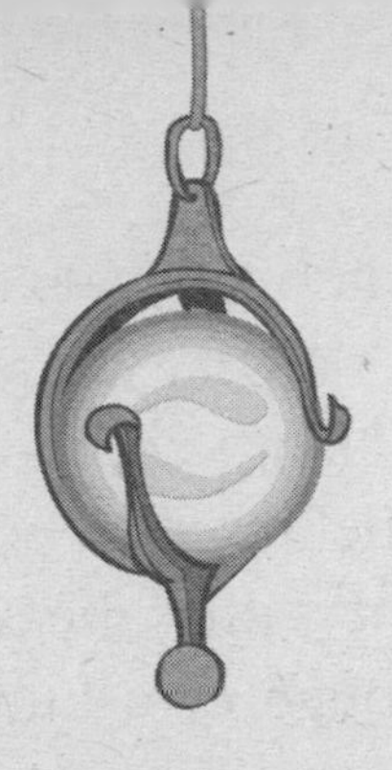

SIX

At the sound of Mrs. Rudolph's voice, Will's heart started thumping wildly, and her mouth went completely dry.

She sounds so *frightened,* Will thought, gripping her cell phone tightly. This must be serious. In all our crazy adventures, we Guardians have freaked out in about a dozen different ways. But, through it all, Mrs. Rudolph has been our rock! She's helped us evade Metamoorian armies and track down portals. She doesn't even get upset when we cringe at her Metamoorian-monster form.

Will couldn't help shuddering when she thought of Mrs. Rudolph's true shape—a rhino-like body covered in brown scales; a smushy, scary face, and bloodred eyes.

At the moment, though, Will could tell that Mrs. Rudolph was in her human form. The key was her voice—it was smooth and throaty instead of gurgly and raspy. But it was also mega-alarmed.

"Thank heavens I found you," Mrs. Rudolph gasped.

"It's an emergency, Will. You have to meet me as soon as you can!"

"What's the matter?" Will asked. She slapped a hand over her ear to block out the noise of students pounding down the hallways and the bell ringing. "Where are you?"

"I'll explain later," Mrs. Rudolph responded breathlessly. "I'll wait for you near the train tracks at Clearview Cross."

"Clearview Cross?" Will sputtered. Having lived in Heatherfield for only a short time, she'd never even heard of the spot.

"I know where it is," Irma said, placing a steady hand on Will's shoulder.

Smiling gratefully at her friend, Will spoke again to Mrs. Rudolph, "Okay, we'll get—"

Skrreeeeeee!

Will yelped and jumped about a foot in the air. A high-pitched and painful screeching had just come out of her phone!

When she'd recovered, she cried, "What was that?"

"Wait a moment, Will," Mrs. Rudolph said over the noise. "A train's passing by—oh, no!"

Will caught her breath.

She waited for Mrs. Rudolph to say something else. Something comforting like, "Oh, no, I just lost one of my boots in the snow." Or: "Oh, no, I almost forgot to tell you to take the crosstown bus, because the Number Twenty-Two was delayed."

Instead, all Will heard was silence.

"Mrs. Rudolph," she squeaked. "Can you hear me? Mrs. Rudolph? Mrs. Rudolph!"

More silence.

"What's wrong, Will?" Irma breathed, her hand tightening on Will's shoulder.

"I'm afraid something terrible just happened!" Will replied, turning her cell off before continuing. "And now, I'm afraid, we've got to get going!"

Within an hour, the Guardians had arrived at Clearview Cross. They found train tracks that led into the stone tunnel. The girls tromped around outside the tunnel looking for clues, apprehensive and confused. There wasn't much to see except for a red phone booth next to a sidewalk blanketed in snow.

The phone booth was empty. What's more, its receiver was dangling off the hook.

At the sight of this desperate-looking scene, Will's heart sank. Suddenly, she spotted something next to the phone booth that made her gasp. Half buried by the steadily falling snowflakes was a woman's hat. It was brown and furry—just the sort of accessory Mrs. Rudolph would wear.

"Is this her hat?" Will asked fearfully, plucking the cap off the ground and shaking off the snow.

"Yes," Cornelia said, glancing over from a few feet away. She pointed at the snow at her feet. "But these sure aren't her footprints!"

Will and the others trotted over to look at Cornelia's discovery. A trail had been cut in the snow by one set of small, human shoes and what looked like the big, bare feet of two, uh, *non*humans. After all, the footprints had only three, pointy toes.

"I don't get it," Irma said, spinning around

to scan the empty hillside once more. "We're at Clearview Cross. We were supposed to meet her here, but there's nobody around!"

"Something must have happened," Will said, trying to keep the mounting panic out of her voice. "Mrs. Rudolph wasn't alone."

"The snowfall's covered some of these footprints," Cornelia observed. Then she looked up and pointed at the stone archway carved into the side of the hill.

"The footsteps lead that way," the blond girl announced.

"A dark, abandoned tunnel," Irma quipped. "Want to go first, Cornelia?"

"Maybe I will, scaredy-cat," Cornelia joked right back. She took a step toward the tunnel—only to be confronted by a terrifying figure, leaping out of the dark interior! Baring long, green talons and even longer teeth, the pointy-eared, green-skinned creature hissed at the Guardians menacingly.

"Aaaaiiiggh!" all five Guardians screamed at once.

Roaring now, the creature began to lunge at the Guardians. It would have made it to them, too, if a hand hadn't reached out of the tunnel and grabbed the monster's shoulder.

It was a human hand—a female one.

It was Mrs. Rudolph's!

Emerging from the shadows, her plump face tense and drawn, Mrs. Rudolph stroked the monster's shoulder.

"No, Alena," she admonished the creature. "These are friends. They're the Guardians of the Veil."

Alena immediately grew calm.

Mrs. Rudolph glanced back into the tunnel and made a beckoning motion. Another creature emerged. This one was slightly taller than Alena. He carried a green infant, swaddled in rags. Will softened. Alena was clearly just a mother, protecting her husband and child.

Now she gazed at the girls with bright, purple eyes.

"Let me introduce you to Alena, Morvan, and their son, Ranni," Mrs. Rudolph said to the girls. "They've just come from Metamoor."

"What were you doing hiding in there?" Irma asked.

"We hid in the tunnel so we wouldn't be seen," Mrs. Rudolph said, stepping further out onto the snow-covered ground. "Am I happy you young ladies showed up!"

"It wasn't easy for us to get here," Will admitted. She handed the brown hat to her teacher. "This must be yours."

Mrs. Rudolph stepped forward to take the hat, then glanced back at the shivering Metamoorians.

"They've had a difficult trip," she sighed to her students. "I was told they would be coming. But something went wrong."

"They didn't come by train, I hope!" Irma said with a grin. "Those things are never on time."

Mrs. Rudolph didn't even crack a smile at Irma's remark.

When someone can completely ignore one of Irma's quips, Will thought with a shiver, things really *are* serious.

"Of course, this family didn't come by train," Mrs. Rudolph said seriously, pointing back at the tunnel. "They crossed through the Veil by way of a portal."

"Wait a second," Hay Lin sputtered, staring at the tunnel's mouth. "That's a portal? My map didn't even warn me!"

Irritably, Hay Lin reached into her coat

pocket and pulled out a folded piece of dusty, yellowed parchment. It was no ordinary map. It was a supernaturally vivid view of Heatherfield. It had been the last gift Hay Lin's grandmother had given her before dying. Whenever the Veil was breached, that portal's location glowed a hot pink on the map.

Just as it was doing at that moment.

"Oh, fantastic," Hay Lin complained, scowling at the map. "Nice alert—after the fact."

"Better late than never," Irma exclaimed with a laugh.

"*As* I said," Mrs. Rudolph said, cutting into Irma's joshing once again. "There was a problem during the family's trip. Alena and Morvan's other son, Reseph, disappeared! He got scared by a freight train passing by and ran off!"

Instantly, Will imagined a little creature—sweet and cute despite the horns on his hairless, green scalp and his clawed feet. He was out wandering the streets of Heatherfield, lost and alone.

"I'm so sorry!" Will cried, hanging her head in despair. "We should have gotten here earlier to help you."

"What's done is done," Mrs. Rudolph said in a practical tone. "Now we have to track Reseph down."

"And that's what we'll do," Will said with a determined nod. "But before we go, we have to take care of the portal."

She looked at her friends, then stared purposefully at the mouth of the tunnel. At the end of the dark corridor, she could see a roiling circle—a doorway formed of shape-shifting clouds and a swirling, silvery substance.

"Right!" Irma realized, falling in behind Will. "We can't leave it open."

Will felt a tiny thrill as her four friends followed her without question, with total trust.

Their trust gave Will the strength to smile as she thrust her arm out in front of her.

"Heart of Candracar!" she cried. "Do your thing!"

When Will opened her fist, the beautiful glass orb was there, hovering above her palm. Blinding rays of pink magic shot out of the amulet, filling the tunnel with a supernatural glow.

Then the Heart beamed a blue teardrop toward Irma. The bubble of power whirled around her, trailing sea-colored magic like a swirl of cotton candy.

"Water!" Irma shouted as the power took effect. She grinned as her limbs began to lengthen; as her hair fell into a smooth, sassy style. Finally, iridescent wings unfurled from Irma's back and her body became covered by a midriff-baring turquoise top, a purple miniskirt, and striped leggings.

The other girls' transformations swiftly followed. Through a fog of sparkles that clouded her vision, Will vaguely heard Cornelia shout, "Earth!" as a cyclone of green magic whirled around her.

"Air!" That was Hay Lin.

"Fire!" Taranee cried.

Finally, it was Will's turn. She felt her torso contract, then stretch back into a graceful arch as she tossed her head backward. With that toss of her head, Will's supersilky hair skimmed her cheek.

Next, Will felt jolts of white-hot energy traveling from her palm to her face, chest, and legs. Her muscles contracted, flexing with new strength.

Finally, Will's wings emerged. She gasped as

she felt the feathers emerge from her back and begin fluttering, making her literally ethereal.

I'm ready, Will thought, gazing at her friends' glamorous, grown-up figures in awe. *We're* ready.

Will motioned to the Guardians to gather around her.

"All together, now!" she ordered.

In perfect synchronicity, the girls thrust out their arms. A bolt of white magic emanated from their palms, shooting toward the portal with such force they all stumbled backward.

Their magical missile might have been harsh, but it worked! The portal exploded with a deafening blast. When the smoke cleared, the silvery, circular doorway had disappeared, replaced by the tunnel's original stone wall.

We did it! Will thought exultantly. Now, on to the next task!

She walked briskly toward Mrs. Rudolph and put a reassuring hand on her teacher's shoulder. Nodding at the couple and baby, she said, "Take these people to a warm, safe place, Mrs. Rudolph."

"We've already figured that out," Mrs. Rudolph assured her. "They'll stay at my house. Once they have changed their appearance, no one will notice them."

No sooner had Mrs. Rudolph spoken these words than the green-skinned mom and dad moved together and huddled close. They closed their eyes and bowed their heads. In a moment, they, too, were swathed in a swirl of sparkling, supernatural power. Theirs was as white as the snow on which they stood.

When Alena and Morvan's magical mist cleared, the creatures' green skin had melted away, replaced by soft, peaches-and-cream complexions. Their scaly scalps had become covered with sand-colored hair. Their eyes went from purple to soft brown and blue. The baby in Morvan's arms began to coo like any other baby, instead of growling.

The only vestige of Alena and Morvan's former selves was the terrified expressions on their faces.

"Reseph doesn't know how to change his appearance," Alena gasped, rushing up to Will to clasp her hands. "He's in danger! Please find him."

"Don't worry," Will heard herself saying with a calmness she didn't quite feel. "Go with

Mrs. Rudolph. We'll start looking for Reseph right away."

Something in Will's face must have reassured the poor mother. She slumped into the crook of her husband's arm with a sigh of relief. The couple let Mrs. Rudolph lead them away.

As Will watched them go, she felt a sudden pang of fear in her gut.

Nice talking, Will, she brooded. But can I actually live up to all my big talk? I totally don't know if I'm up for this!

Will felt despair welling up inside her. But then, she spotted something—something that gave her hope. Dotting the hill from the tunnel's mouth up to the crest were footprints. They were half buried in new snow, but they were clear enough for Will to discern a claw shape, with three pointy, reptilian toes.

"Reseph!" Will breathed. She began to clamber up the hillside. Her friends chased after her—until she came to an abrupt halt. She tore her gaze away from the trail.

The trail had stopped at some train tracks that overlooked a dense, urban neighborhood, bustling with cars, bicycles, and busy commuters.

"He must have crossed the tracks," Will sighed, gazing down at the city.

"We have to come up with a plan to find him," Taranee said, realizing how much distance they had to cover in their search.

"Yeah!" Will agreed with a sigh. "But where do we start?"

The four friends turned and looked at Will expectantly.

Oh, yeah, Will thought with a shrug. I almost forgot. The leader is supposed to *answer* these questions, not ask them.

So she shrugged and said, "Let's go back to my house. My mom won't be home from work for hours. We can make a plan there."

Well, we can *try* and make a plan here, Will sighed, a half hour later. The girls were gathered around her dining-room table, where Hay Lin had spread out the map of the portals.

As usual, though, the map gave Will no answers at all. It only raised more questions.

"He could be anywhere!" she exclaimed in frustration. "And with every minute that passes, the situation just gets worse and worse."

Staring at the map, Will shivered. In her

Guardian guise she'd been impervious to the snowy cold, and focused completely on the mission at hand. Now, after shifting back into her usual body, dressed in her woolly red sweater, she felt a chill. Maybe the wintry weather was to blame. Or maybe it was Will's concern for little Reseph.

"We'll have to split up," she declared, shaking her head at the breadth of Heatherfield's map. It seemed to be the only logical solution. "If only we had a clue where to look, or how to help that little boy."

"The only place we can get all the answers," Hay Lin piped up from her seat at the table, "is Candracar!"

"Then maybe we'd better find a way to get there," Irma said.

Will looked over at Irma to see if she were serious or if this were another one of her friend's constant jokes. After all, Candracar was as distant and mystical as heaven. And, to Will at least, it seemed just as unreachable.

"My grandmother told me about Candracar once," Hay Lin noted. "To get there, you have to cross over an air-colored bridge."

Oh, well, then, that should be super-easy,

Will thought sarcastically, her shoulders slumping. Now Candracar seemed just *so* much more accessible.

Will flopped dejectedly into a chair. But once again, an internal tugging stopped her. It might have been the Heart of Candracar, speaking to Will's subconscious. More likely, it was her famous stubborn streak rearing its head.

You know what? Will thought suddenly. I've discovered portals to Metamoor and monsters in closets. How much harder can an air-colored bridge be? I'm gonna track it down and get some answers.

"Okay!" she said, pushing her chair away and heading for the front door. "Let's go find that bridge."

"Are you kidding?" Cornelia sputtered, leaping up from the table.

"You don't know what you're talking about," Hay Lin said, sharing Cornelia's disbelief.

"You're right!" Will declared angrily. She spun around to face her friends. "I don't know! I don't know *anything*. And I can't take it any more."

Will felt her lower lip tremble. But the last thing she wanted to do just then was to burst into tears of frustration. Instead, she walked over to the window, avoiding her friends' concerned looks in favor of gazing out at Heatherfield's snowy streets.

"We have a map that only works when we don't need it," Will said. "We have powers we barely understand and we have an impossible mission. Now a little boy from Metamoor has disappeared to who-knows-where. I don't *want* to take it anymore."

Taranee joined Will at the window.

"If you're going to Candracar," she said somberly, "I'm going with you."

"Hmmm, a place with all the answers, huh?" Irma piped up, pretending to ponder the decision. "Well, that means they'll have the answers to my French test!"

Will turned to gaze at her friends. All of them were nodding. They were all going with her! She really was becoming a leader.

She motioned her friends over to the loft's big, red couch. They sat in a tight circle as Will lifted her hand, releasing the beaming Heart of Candracar from her palm almost effortlessly.

"Let's concentrate," she instructed her friends. There was no time for hesitating.

We are Guardians, Will thought. *We can do this if we try. I know it!*

Out loud, she addressed the glowing amulet hovering above her hand: "Heart of *Candracar*—that's exactly where you're going to take us!"

SEVEN

The Oracle floated in the center of a spherical room. Unlike some of the chambers in the Temple of Candracar, which loomed for miles into the air, this globe-shaped haven was small and cozy. Its walls were etched with hieroglyphics illustrating Candracar's history, a story that extended back to a time when the universe had first begun to take shape.

It was there, inside that small room, that the Oracle would gather the strength he needed to oblige the Guardians' request.

Their summons—emitted with a great burst of energy from the Heart of Candracar—had hit the Oracle with all the force of a lightning bolt. It had even weakened him slightly—at least, in the physical sense.

But the diminutive man's spirit had not been shaken by that impudent interruption. The Oracle was peace personified. Though the Oracle was thousands of years old, his face was smooth and unlined. His wisdom was boundless.

He was smiling now as he folded his legs beneath him, assuming a perfect lotus position atop a hovering pocket of air. He turned his head toward a platform that extended like a scallop shell from the chamber's arched door.

On that ledge stood Tibor, the Oracle's faithful adviser. As usual, his expression was the exact opposite of his master's. While the Oracle's glowing countenance was suffused with calm, Tibor's face was furrowed in consternation. The ancient adviser's long, snow-white beard shook in agitation as he addressed his master.

"This is unheard of, Oracle," Tibor declared. "No Guardian has ever dared such a feat before. What do you intend to do about it?"

"Nothing," the Oracle said. "I will do nothing, and this will please the Council of Elders. I believe they've grown very fond of the girls."

The Oracle's smile faded and was replaced

by an expression of calm concentration. He extracted his hands from deep within his silken robe's bell-like sleeves.

"Their request for knowledge is legitimate," the Oracle said to Tibor.

The Oracle had spoken. There was no need for him to defend his decision any further.

When next he spoke, no sound came from his lips. Instead, his message was transmitted—in the form of pure, golden energy—down to earth and to his five Guardians.

If you've made up your minds, girls, if you are really ready for the truth . . .

The Oracle received vibrations back from the Guardians—affirmations that the five girls did not even know they were sending to the Oracle.

The Oracle closed his eyes. Now, he could see the girls clearly. They were at Will's home, sitting in a tight circle. Their hands were clasped, except for Will's; her palm was outstretched, cupping the Heart of Candracar. The amulet transmitted all the girls' hopes and dreams directly to the Oracle.

Yes, the Oracle would answer their request. He sent a mist of sunlight, blue shadows, and soporific dust into the girls' minds.

Yes, he thought. As images began to take shape in his head, the very same images formed in the minds of the Guardians.

Yes, the Oracle repeated, granting the girls their wishes. He would provide them with answers—answers to questions they didn't even know they were asking. *Your hopes. And the truth. They are all in your dreams. . . .*

EIGHT

Irma was sitting at her desk in French class.

How she was sitting in her desk in French class, she didn't know. She'd just left the class a few hours ago—after an excruciating exam, she might have added.

Maybe, Irma thought blearily, all that hard thinking has fogged my brain.

She blinked groggily at her classmates, who seemed to be floating in a bluish fog. As usual, they were laughing, talking, and scribbling in their notebooks. But this morning? This after-noon? Whatever time it was—they moved in slow motion, as if they were walking through water.

Madame Gounod seemed to be moving in a graceful haze. Well, she was as graceful as her angular body and shellacked, bouffant hairdo would allow. She undulated toward Irma.

"Here's your French test, Irma," the teacher said.

Irma squeezed her hands together on top of her desk and bowed her head, wishing she could summon her magic. Not that it could help her now.

What she really wanted to do was wish that moment away completely, like a genie who had absolute powers.

"As-tu compris Français?" Madame Gounod demanded, jolting Irma from the watery world of her thoughts. She thrust Irma's French test at her. It was slashed with thick red *x*'s and cross-outs, and even some angry scribbles. Irma could barely make out the purple ink of her own multiple-choice *x*'s and lengthy translations through all the red markings.

"Français," Madame Gounod continued, "is *not* the language you used on this page!" Her voice was somehow shrill and garbled at the same time.

Oh, no! Irma thought with a sigh. There goes the school play!

A moment later, Irma found herself in one of the school's hallways. And, once again, how she'd gotten there she had no idea. But she had the strange sensation that she'd floated out of the room, buoyed up, perhaps, by the wavery jangling of the school bell.

"M—maybe, now," Irma whispered to herself, "I'll wake up, and all of this will have been just a bad dream."

Yes . . . a dream. . . .

Irma heard the voice in the back of her head. It was so whispery it was almost impossible to make out.

And yet she could make it out. A voice was definitely speaking to Irma. It sounded muffled and remote, as if it were coming through a thick barrier of water.

"This is a dream," Irma whispered in awe. She gazed with new interest around the shadowy halls of her school. Her classmates continued to undulate through the corridors like bits of seaweed floating in the sea.

One of them wore a puffy coat, long, blue-black pigtails, and endearingly goofy leg warmers bunched down around her calves. Hay Lin was in her dream!

"So, Irma?" Hay Lin said with a pleasant smile.

"Bad news," Irma drawled. "It doesn't look like I'll be able to take part in your play."

"That's strange," Hay Lin said, her face becoming thoughtful. Looking at her friend through that blue tint made her seem ghostly and far away.

"My grandma," Hay Lin continued, "said the same thing in my dream last night."

Wake up.

Irma looked around, as if searching for the annoying source of a pestering gnat's buzz. Except that the buzz was that whispery voice again. It was reedy and shaky, and it seemed to be made even shakier by great age and great distance. Irma knew the voice, yet she couldn't place it.

"And then, Grandma said she wasn't happy with me," Hay Lin continued as the girls walked down the corridor toward one of the glass doors. The sunlight reflecting off the snow outside shone through the doors, breaking into the hallway's shadowy haze like a spotlight. "She doesn't like the way I behave."

Hay Lin threw open the doors and stepped

out onto the front steps, breathing in the crisp, winter air with delight. Irma blinked at her slowly, like a fish gazing out from its tank. Why couldn't she share in Hay Lin's exuberance? Why was everything dulled?

Had Irma felt more clearheaded, she might have stopped to wonder how she was taking part in what was clearly Hay Lin's dream—and why Hay Lin was bopping around in hers.

But that's the thing with dreams, isn't it? Irma thought, waggling her fingers with exaggerated slowness in front of her foggy eyes. Everything—and nothing—makes sense.

Awaken. . . .

Irma looked up. But Hay Lin simply continued to gaze ahead, breathing in the winter chill. Apparently, she hadn't heard the whispery voice.

"Grandma might be disappointed," she said, standing lightly on her tiptoes. "But I just can't resist this fresh air and the idea of a little flying!"

Like a leaf suddenly carried into the air by a breeze, Hay Lin was lifted off the ground. She threw her head back and extended her arms gracefully behind her. Her pigtails rippled around her waist like silken ribbons.

She skimmed over the heads of the Sheffielders who were tromping through the school's front lawn or throwing snowballs. Soon, she started swooping in little circles.

She was giddily, unapologetically, magical.

"I love this feeling!" she called down to Irma.

"Can you see Will from up there?" Irma called back. But Hay Lin was too far away to hear Irma—or simply didn't care to answer. She headed for the archway that guarded Sheffield Institute from the outside world.

Irma gazed at her friend wistfully.

Can you hear me?

Irma wanted to answer the voice. She really did. But before she could focus her bleary mind on the whispery question, something distracted her. It was Will. She was riding her bike on the sidewalk just outside the Sheffield Institute arch.

"Wilma!" Irma cried. There was a note of desperation in her own voice that irritated her. But Irma was so relieved to see Will that she didn't stop to contemplate it. She tromped down the walkway and burst through the arched doorway to wave frantically at her friend.

"Irma!" Will admonished her. She brought her bike to a skidding halt and gazed nervously around her. "Don't call me that. How many times do I have to tell you? I don't want anyone to find out my real name!"

Hay Lin suddenly swooped down to hover over Will and Irma, who was feeling a sudden, apologetic pang in her belly.

"Are we going to the movies this afternoon?" Hay Lin asked her two friends.

Movies? Irma thought. Like the movie I'm living? The one I want to change?

"Only," Will said with a wink, "if we pick a romantic one! Make sure you let Cornelia and Taranee know."

Irma nodded emphatically. Or at least, she tried to. But her head felt heavy.

Will didn't seem to notice. She simply waved good-bye and began to pedal away, artfully dodging patches of ice and tiny hills of snow as she made her way down the sidewalk.

Irma waved at Will's back. Her friend was growing smaller as she rode into the distance, but she never seemed to disappear over a crest in the sidewalk or around a corner, the way she would have in real life.

Irma waved yet again. Even as she did it, though, she knew her friendly send-off was false. She didn't want Will to go. She wanted to hang on to her! She needed her!

Yet Irma waved and waved some more.

What I really need, she thought, is to wake up, to emerge from this murky dream.

NINE

Will felt out of sorts as she rode off on her bike. Part of her expected that she wouldn't be able to get away; that an invisible thread running between her and her friends would suddenly stretch to its limit and pull her back.

As Will kept pedaling, she was vaguely aware of the buildings around her, basking in a faint, pink light. Will looked into the sky, searching the foggy atmosphere for the light source.

There was none. The sky was sunless.

It was then that Will began to realize something.

Maybe this isn't real, she thought. Maybe I'm dreaming these actions, instead of living them.

But what had brought her to this dream? Will couldn't remember going to sleep. She couldn't even remember her day coming to an end. All she could conjure up from the past few hours was the feeling of fervently wishing for something. But this was no birthday-candle type of wish. This was a serious desire. But what was it? What did Will want?

I'd like for things with Mom to go better, Will thought, though she suspected that that wasn't what she'd been asking for. I want to be the one to make my own decisions.

But, on the other hand, she realized suddenly, I'm afraid of doing everything all by myself.

She palled at the idea of a life without her mother telling her what to do.

That truth upset Will, *and* it comforted her at the same time. Most of all, it made Will want to share with her mother her burden—her identity as leader of the Guardians of the Veil.

She'd never believe it, Will thought, closing her eyes for a moment. Lately, she and her mom had been battling constantly. It was out of control! Her mom thought she was just your average, sulky, rebellious teenager.

And that wasn't the only one of her relationships that was in danger. Will began focusing on someone else, adding him to her mental wish list.

If only Matt didn't hate me, she thought morosely. She thought about her crush and about how that was totally not working out as she'd wanted.

Swish, swish, swish, went her bicycle pedals as Will imagined Matt's sweet face. Will's crush on the shaggy-haired lead singer of Cobalt Blue had been disastrous from the start, when Will had bonked Matt on the foot. She'd thought he was the person persecuting a scared little dormouse in the woods.

She'd been wrong, of course. It was a gang of other boys that had been tormenting the critter. Matt—the grandson of a veterinarian—had helped Will rescue the dormouse and encouraged her to take it home as a pet. Later, when Will had been away in Metamoor, Matt had taken care of the dormouse for her.

And then, look what happened, Will thought with another cringe. My astral drop—the loopy double I left behind to cover for my absence—kissed Matt. On the lips! To make matters worse, once she realized how much she'd messed up, the astral drop slapped him across the face in front of everyone at Sheffield Institute!

Sure, Matt had been a little friendly since the incident. But Will knew deep down that he'd have prefered someone older, someone cooler, someone more like—Will's bewitching Guardian self! But she wasn't allowed to show Matt—or anyone—her magical side.

There's no getting around it, Will thought with a sigh. *Matt is as far away from my world as—as my dad is from my mom's!*

Dad! Will thought dreamily. *If only Dad were still with us.*

Though the thought of her dad made Will feel superwistful, her legs were as sprightly as ever. They were pumping her bike pedals with extra sureness. Will couldn't imagine what was causing that burst of strength. Perhaps it was her anger and frustration.

Or maybe, Will thought, gazing around her as her lank hair flapped in the wind, *all this pink light is giving me power—like the glow from the Heart of Candracar.*

The glow was pulling Will through her

dream. Will hoped it was drawing her closer to her wish for a life with a boyfriend, and a father, and a family, once again.

Careful what you wish for, Will. . . .

Will heard a whispery voice in the back of her mind. It was reedy, creaky, and somehow familiar. Will wondered where she'd heard the voice before. Perhaps in another dream? Or a nightmare?

. . . Because you just might get your wish.

Will frowned and waved a hand next to her ear as if to shoo away a bug. Then she swooshed into the parking lot of her building and went inside.

Still feeling strangely buoyant, Will decided to take the stairs up to her apartment, rather than wait for the elevator. But when she reached the base of the stairwell, she stopped in her tracks.

At the top of the stairs, two people were standing at her own front door. One was her mother, standing in the doorframe, looking sad and forlorn. Her pretty face was paler than usual, framed by her long, dark hair.

The other person was Mom's boyfriend—*and* Will's history teacher—Mr. Collins.

The two adults looked as though they were on the verge of tears.

Will shrank back so they wouldn't see her. She knew she just should walk away, but she couldn't help gazing up at the couple.

Up until that moment, Will had felt one thing, and one thing only, about the thought of her Mom and Mr. Collins together—*ewww!*

But now, as she watched Mr. Collins clasp her mother's hands, Will didn't feel disgusted at all. She leaned in closer to listen.

"We've already discussed this," Mr. Collins was saying to her mother in a sad voice. "I *can't* turn down the transfer."

"Then," Mom replied with a catch in her voice, "it's over?"

Mr. Collins's answer was clear as he put his arms around Will's mother, apparently for the very last time.

"Good-bye, Susan," he choked. "Take care of yourself."

Even from her spot at the base of the stairs, Will could see the tears spilling down her mother's cheeks.

"It's not fair!" Mom wept.

Will was shocked. She was so stunned that

she almost forgot to hide when Mr. Collins pulled away from her mother and began to plod down the stairs, wiping his teary eyes with the back of his hand.

Finally, though, she came to her senses.

I'd better hurry before they see me, she thought. She moved with magical lightness away from the staircase. Hiding in the pink-tinted shadows, she watched Mr. Collins stumble through the front door of the building.

I didn't think, Will thought haltingly. *I didn't know . . .*

She would have gone on brooding in confusion, but that whispery voice returned, butting in to her thoughts.

You have to wake up now, it said.

Will heard the voice and nodded vaguely. But she was powerless to wake up; powerless to do anything but drift up the stairs and into her mother's sad embrace.

"I'm sorry, Mom," Will whispered as her mother wept quietly on her shoulder.

"I know, Will," Mom rasped. "I know."

Will was caught up in a flood of emotions—sympathy, yearning, anxiety, and that magical lightness. She had the sense that she was on the cusp of something, something amazing.

Click.

Will pulled her face away from her mother's heaving shoulders to turn and look at the door. A man had just walked through it. He had a thick shock of red hair that was going gray at the temples. His face was kind and seemed tired. In each of his hands was a suitcase.

"Susan. Will," the man said. His voice wobbled with emotion.

"Dad!" Will cried, incredulously.

Finally, all her strange feelings were beginning to make sense. She must have known that she was going to be able to launch herself into her father's arms when he walked through the door, when he returned home, to his family!

"You came back!" Will cried, wrapping her arms around her father's neck, squeezing so hard he grunted.

"Look how my little girl has grown!" Dad said, love and laughter choking his voice.

Will couldn't speak. She was too moved, too happy. She merely squeezed her Dad around the ribs and gazed up at him.

Mom gazed at him, too. Will's parents' distance, their pain, even Mr. Collins, seemed to have melted away in an instant. Mom's eyes were soft as she said to Dad, "We were about to have dinner. Will you join us?"

Will wanted to live in that moment forever. She refused to believe she couldn't. Metamoor, air-colored bridges, Candracar—it was all receding into a breezy, pink haze in the back of her mind.

That's enough, Will. You have to wake up. . . .

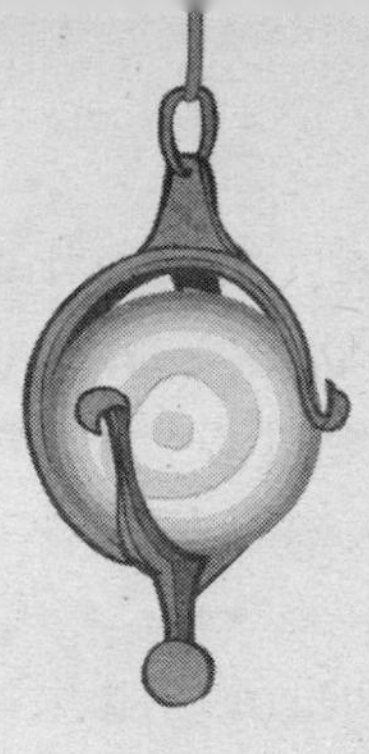

TEN

Cornelia was standing outside a familiar house, gazing up at its snow-frosted roof through the branches of a few pine trees. She had no idea how she'd gotten there.

And for some strange reason, she didn't care.

Whoa, Cornelia thought. What's wrong with this picture? Am I dreaming or what?

Glancing to her left, she saw beautiful, light-bedecked trees. On her right—

Cornelia gasped.

Now I *know* I'm definitely dreaming, she thought, feeling a little lightheaded.

She turned to her right again. There was Peter Cook. And he wasn't just standing next to her. *He was holding her hand!* Their fingers were cozily intertwined.

Cornelia gazed in awe at Peter's chiseled face and his sweet, expectant smile. He was gazing up at a gable in the roof, with twin windows and a pretty arch.

This was a dream house, as warm and inviting as Cornelia's own penthouse apartment was cool and sleek.

She squeezed Peter's warm hand. He squeezed back, then glanced at her playfully with wide brown eyes.

Well, guess what? Cornelia thought recklessly. If this is a dream, I'm gonna go with it! This is a good one!

Girls . . . it's time for all of you to wake up. Wake up.

Cornelia shook her head as a whispery little voice, an annoying one at that, began buzzing in the back of her mind.

She didn't really want to think about being one of the girls just then. She wanted only to go into the warm house and enjoy being with Peter, whose strong arm was pressing against her own with a reassuring weight.

Peter was solid. He was normal. And, most of all, he was there.

Well, *there* is a relative term, Cornelia mused, gazing around at what was clearly her dream landscape. The evening air was filled with a pretty, green glow, as if the moon actually *were* made of green cheese.

Just like I used to wish when I was a little girl, Cornelia thought. Tonight, it looks as if all my wishes are coming true.

I think I know what I'm doing here! Cornelia thought as she gazed up at the house's arched window.

Cornelia cupped a hand around her mouth and called up to the window.

"Get down here, lazybones!" she hollered in her loudest voice.

Peter chuckled.

A head appeared in the window. Cornelia was not surprised to find herself gazing up at Elyon!

Her old friend's cornsilk-colored, shaggy braids and elfin face were unmistakable. But the best part was that Elyon's Metamoorian wardrobe—long, dour robes emblazoned with the sinister green Seal of Phobos—was gone. Elyon was wearing a purple fleece hoodie over an orange T-shirt. She looked like what she used to be—a sweet, grinning, teenage girl. And Cornelia's best friend.

"I'll come down there," she yelled from the corner window, "but only if you stop yelling. Gosh, Peter. Your girlfriend can be *so* rude sometimes!"

Girlfriend! Cornelia thought with an inward thrill. Wow. I'm Peter's girlfriend? Nothing can wreck this momen—

"Are you still talking to that traitor?"

Cornelia groaned.

I had to go and jinx myself, she sighed. She glanced over her shoulder to see Taranee glaring at her.

Taranee's feet, in her clunky boots, were planted in the snow. Her hands were curled into fists and her eyes were narrowed to surly slits. She was practically breathing fire, she was so mad.

"What's gotten into you, little sister?" Peter asked Taranee innocently.

"Yeah," Cornelia echoed with a nonchalant shrug. "We already talked about this, Taranee. Elyon is our friend. What happened is over and done with."

Cornelia felt a tiny twinge of guilt as she

said the words. What had happened to Taranee as a result of Elyon's actions—kidnapping and some serious head games—was far worse than anything the other four Guardians had suffered. After the Guardians had arrived and helped her escape from Elyon's glass cage, Taranee had recovered from her trauma. But she'd never forgiven Elyon.

That was clear as Taranee yelled at Cornelia in the green-dappled haze of Elyon's dreamy front lawn.

"She put us right into Cedric's hands!" Taranee reminded Cornelia. "She tried to get rid of us! Don't you see that Elyon is not a real friend to us anymore?"

Cornelia shrugged again and glanced up at the arched window. Elyon was still there, grinning impudently. She was the old Elyon, from her smiling face to her casual and breezing banter.

But Taranee—a Sheffield newbie who hadn't even known Elyon that long before she had disappeared—would not have recognized that. She wasn't like Cornelia, yearning for a past friendship and dreaming about what a good friend Elyon had been to her.

Taranee was nothing but angry.

"Why do you keep making excuses for Elyon?" she demanded of Cornelia. Her question ended in a high-pitched shriek. Taranee's fists suddenly erupted into great balls of flame. The most mild-mannered of the five Guardians had become a rage machine, as fiery and dangerous as a vengeful dragon.

As Cornelia gaped at her friend, the whispery voice returned. It had stopped issuing orders. Now it was buzzing around her brain with a steady chant in a language Cornelia had never heard.

Li kun tui kin kannnnnn . . .

Cornelia held out her hands and tried to counter Taranee's hot, orange magic with blasts of her own cool, green kind. But Taranee was a fellow Guardian. Her power equaled Cornelia's. And in this nightmare, fire beat earth. Cornelia watched as Taranee turned toward Elyon's house—

Ken chen li kun tui kien kan. Ken chen . . .

Taranee reared back, putting all the strength she had into creating the fireballs. The flames were separating from her hands now—

Sun li kun . . .

Cornelia tried to scream. But she couldn't form any words. She could barely breathe.

SUNNN! LI KUNNN TUI KIEN KANNNNN!

Taranee hurled the fireballs at the house. One hit the front door with a dreadful *whooosh*. Another ignited the snow-dappled shrubs. Taranee's aim wasn't perfect, but the fireballs were creating a fiery disaster.

Another sailed up into the corner window where Elyon stood.

Cornelia choked on her own panicked breath. She watched in horror as Elyon disappeared, enveloped by ten-foot-tall flames.

As she tried to run toward the house, Peter grabbed her and dragged her away.

SUNNN! LI KUNNN TUI KIEN KANNNNN!

Taranee hurled more and more vicious, angry heat at the house.

Girls!

Cornelia only wanted to leave this moment, to wake up from this horrible, frightening nightmare!

It's time to wake up!

Yes, Cornelia thought. Her own voice echoed hollowly against the inside of her skull as she and Peter fled Elyon's burning home.

Yes, it's time to wake up. I don't want to see this anymore.

Open your eyes. . . .

With a sigh of relief, Cornelia obeyed the command in her head. She opened her eyes—her nightmare had ended.

ELEVEN

Hay Lin was flying. She knew that she wasn't supposed to be. The schoolyard below her was teeming with Sheffielders who were *not* supposed to find out about her special flying powers.

What was more, Hay Lin was supposed to use those powers for saving the world—not for having fun!

A reedy voice in the back of Hay Lin's head had been telling her as much. It had been urging her to wake up from her breezy, swoopy dream, speaking to her in warm cadences that felt eerily familiar.

Still, Hay Lin couldn't quite place the sound of the voice.

She also refused to heed it.

She kept flying, soaring higher and higher.

The voice began to chant in an ancient Asian language Hay Lin knew from her family's rituals. Her grandmother had chanted like that when she'd said her prayers.

Yes—her grandmother—

Ken chen li kun tui kien kan . . . the voice chanted. *Ken chen LI KUN TUI KIEN KAN* . . .

After a few moments, the chants faded away. They were replaced, once again, by orders in their own language. The voice admonished not just Hay Lin, but all five Guardians of the Veil.

Girls! It's time to wake up! Open your eyes. . . . Come, now. Open your eyes.

With a sigh of resignation, Hay Lin finally obeyed. She slowly descended and came to a stop on the ground. She blinked several times and looked around, squinting. A rainbow-tinted light was almost blinding her with its brightness.

Hay Lin was completely disoriented!

She found herself sprawled on a surface that wasn't quite a surface. It was both smooth and soft. Hay Lin noticed that circles emanated from the spot where she sat—like the ripples created by a stone dropped into the still water of a lake.

Is that where I am? In a body of water? Hay Lin wondered.

She stumbled to her feet, conscious as she stretched out her sleepy body that she was back in her Guardian form.

Hay Lin noticed, with a sigh of relief, that her friends were sprawled around her, too. She watched as Irma, Will, Taranee, and Cornelia slowly rubbed their eyes and stretched. They were all awakening, all with the same confused looks on their faces—looks that questioned both where they were and where they'd been.

Nothing we just experienced, Hay Lin realized suddenly, was real. It was all just in our heads. And now, we're waking up to a reality that's weirder than any dream.

"What the—" Will was saying as she stumbled to her feet and looked around. When she saw that, in her purple boots, she was standing on a surface both clear and cloudy, solid and transparent, her eyes widened.

"This is the bridge to Candracar!" she exclaimed. "The air-colored bridge."

Li kun tui kien kan ken chen sunnnnn . . .

The chanting that had buzzed in the back of each Guardian's mind suddenly burst forth in the air around them. The voice was high-pitched and reedy, but also confident and strong.

"That's my grandmother's voice!" Hay Lin cried out happily.

Instantly, tears sprang to her eyes. Since her grandmother had passed away, Hay Lin had missed her constantly.

But now, Grandma was there!

Or was she?

Hay Lin heard the old woman's voice and felt her presence—larger than life—looking kindly down upon the girls.

But Hay Lin couldn't actually see her beloved grandmother.

Almost as if she could sense Hay Lin's confusion, her grandmother now said, "Here, nothing is as it seems!"

As her voice boomed through the sky, it seemed to make the clouds shimmer. The presence of Hay Lin's grandmother surrounded the girls, even though she wasn't there in material form. Her presence was felt by all of the Guardians.

Hay Lin let out an involuntary sob. Happiness, relief, and even grief were swirling around inside her. But, as her grandmother continued to speak, Hay Lin quickly calmed down. Her grandmother's wisdom had always had that effect on her. And she felt that her grandmother had something important to say to all of them.

"You have demonstrated great strength," the elderly lady intoned from the heavens. "You have emerged from a place where desires and fears become real!"

"Incredible," Cornelia breathed, gazing into the pink-and-blue sky and down at the transparent bridge.

"Desires and fears made real," Will murmured. "But then, what about Mr. Collins? And my father?"

"That was only a dream, Will," Hay Lin explained to her friend gently. "Like my sensation of flying."

"Peter," Cornelia said suddenly, looking down at her feet. "And Elyon. They were just illusions, too."

Taranee didn't speak. She simply looked at her hands in troubled wonder.

Gazing at her friends' sad faces, Hay Lin felt sure that their dreams had been just as profound—and troubling—as her own. Then she remembered why they were really there. For answers! She stopped thinking about the dreams.

Again, her grandmother seemed to know the Guardians' desires before they'd voiced them. And again, she began to speak.

"I will tell you the story of the Veil, beginning at the beginning!" Hay Lin's grandmother announced.

Hay Lin spotted something out of the corner of her eye. A series of large, translucent green panels was floating toward the girls. The panels were arranged in two straight lines. As they got closer, Hay Lin could see beautiful pictures on them.

So this is what school is like in Candracar, Hay Lin thought with a slight smile. That's one high-tech blackboard!

"Come closer," her grandmother ordered. The Guardians clustered together as the first massive panel slid into place before them. It hovered at eye-level. Its image of two planets—one enormous and one small—glowed and throbbed with green light. Hay Lin noticed that the planets were rotating slightly. This was the coolest visual aid ever!

"The Veil," her grandmother began, "was created to defend the rest of the universe from the threat of Metamoor. The ancient, wise beings of Candracar put up the barrier as we waited for the Light of Meridian to rise to her full power and illuminate that dark world."

The panel slid silently away. It was replaced by one featuring a picture of a wise-looking girl with straw-colored braids and an impishly pointy chin. She gazed at the girls from beneath a halo of green flames.

"Elyon!" Will whispered. Then she looked up at Hay Lin's grandmother. "She's the 'Light of Meridian,' Metamoor's savior?"

"Her arrival," Hay Lin's grandmother said, nodding her head in confirmation, "would reestablish balance. Until then, Guardians were to be assigned to watch over the Veil, to protect the fragile border."

A new panel hummed into view. This one showed a familiar-looking, reptilian monster, erupting with a giant roar from a swirling portal.

Standing before him, five girls with purple

and turquoise gowns and iridescent wings faced him down with bolts of magic. One of them—with long pigtails and a widow's peak—looked remarkably like Hay Lin!

That must be my grandmother when she was a young Guardian, Hay Lin realized with a gasp. *She told me right before she died that she'd been a Guardian, too. But it had always been hard to picture my tiny old grandma, doing battle with Metamoorian baddies. Guess I was wrong. She was a total toughie! And* I *have to follow in her footsteps. Can I really do this?*

Grandmother's next words were not especially reassuring.

"The most difficult task of all," Hay Lin's grandmother said, "has now been entrusted to you. You have to protect a Veil that has grown old and fallen into decay. And you have to protect Meridian's only hope from the evil plans of Prince Phobos."

The last panel hovered before the girls. A young man with Elyon's pale hair and honey-colored skin glared out at the girls from behind a thicket of black roses. A turquoise crown rested on his long hair. The cap formed a sinister point between his blue eyes. He had a red goatee that was combed to a sheen, and his thin-lipped mouth was grim. It was Phobos, the prince of Metamoor.

Hay Lin had seen Metamoorian villains that were a lot scarier than this dude. But she knew enough about Phobos to surmise that his handsomeness was part of his evil, his ability to deceive.

The sight of Phobos made the girls' mission clear to them again. Hay Lin reached into her striped, turquoise kneesock. When she was in her earthling form, the precious Heatherfield map was usually stashed in her backpack or coat pocket. As a Guardian, Hay Lin kept the folded paper tucked into her sock.

She unfurled the map and looked into the heavens, imagining that she was gazing into her grandmother's calm, black eyes.

"If we have to do such a difficult task," she asked, "then why give us such unreliable tools to do the job?"

"My little one," her grandmother crooned, bringing another lump to Hay Lin's throat. "It is not by following a map that you will accomplish your mission. You have faced danger with courage and loyalty. Those are your tools. By trying to reach Candracar by yourself, you have proved that you are ready."

She uttered this last statement with such power and assurance that Hay Lin felt certain the other members of the Congregation of Candracar supported her claim. She could picture her grandmother standing in a dazzling temple decorated with art from floor to ceiling, with friends all around her. A dazzling window formed in front of her.

Through that window, Hay Lin's grandmother's invisible hand suddenly reached down and plucked the map from Hay Lin's hands. As the map floated up and over Hay Lin's head, the parchment burst into flames. In mere seconds, the dusty, dry map had disintegrated, becoming a scattering of dust and a wisp of sweet-smelling smoke.

The ancient map that Hay Lin had guarded so carefully all those months was gone in an instant.

"That map," the wise old lady informed the girls, "was just one step on the road to understanding." She turned to smile at the Guardians her eyes shining. "Now, think of it no more, and return to Heatherfield."

Suddenly, the clouds that had cushioned the air-colored bridge parted. With her friends, Hay Lin tentatively peeked through the small opening.

She gasped.

There was her hometown, arrayed before her like, well, like the image of it on the map that had just disappeared from her grasp. From her ethereal vantage point, Hay Lin could see all of her favorite places.

There was the lighthouse that beckoned her home whenever she and her dad went out sailing. There was Shell Cave on the beach, where she and Irma had spent many hours picnicking, playing, and drawing pictures on the walls. And there was the Silver Dragon, her parents' Chinese restaurant and her home. Hay Lin felt a pang of longing for the familiar, laughter-filled dinner in her family's cozy apartment over the restaurant.

Maybe, Hay Lin thought wistfully, I'll see Mom and Dad soon—if, and only if, we're able to complete this particular mission. We are Guardians of the Veil!

Once again reading her granddaughter's

thoughts, Grandma's reedy voice filled the air with a gentle order.

"Go down there now," she said to the Guardians. "Reseph is in danger. He needs you. Look for him at the dog pound. I will show you the way!"

TWELVE

As the voice of Hay Lin's grandmother echoed in her head, Will squared her shoulders.

As shaky and unsure as she had felt in her loft a few hours ago, that was how confident she felt now. She'd done something miraculous. She, with the help of the Heart of Candracar, of course, had spirited her friends to a place that she hadn't even fully believed in—the air-colored bridge to Candracar.

I can't believe, Will thought, that our mission has gotten even bigger. I mean, I thought guarding the Veil and closing the portals was a big deal. Now I learn we've also got to help the Light of Meridian—as in, Elyon—ascend to power and defeat her all-powerful brother?

The mountainous burden made Will's

winged shoulders sag a bit.

But only a bit. The clarity of that heavenly air, not to mention the confidence surging through her mind, helped Will refocus on the slightly more manageable task at hand—tracking down a lost little Metamoorian boy and returning him to his worried parents.

Will was determined to succeed.

No sooner had that thought crossed her mind than the girls were suddenly whooshed away from the bridge, and away from the place they'd worked so hard to reach.

It happened so fast Will barely had time to take a breath. Suddenly, she found herself on a bustling Heatherfield street, flanked by her fellow Guardians.

Huh! Will thought with a dry laugh. *That was abrupt. Sort of like becoming a Guardian in the first place. It's not like we had any warning about that, either.*

Had she had the time, Will might have settled in for a little post-Candracar brooding. But the girls didn't have a moment to lose. Will could only imagine what terrified little Reseph might have experienced since being separated suddenly from his parents.

She pictured him draped in a rough, brown, hooded cloak. He stumbled, she imagined, onto a narrow street in downtown Heatherfield that was lined with sparkling shops. The street would be bustling with people, smiling as they did their holiday shopping.

Everywhere, Reseph would see tall people whisking by in brightly colored scarves and hats. He'd smell the unfamiliar scents of hot cocoa and coffee wafting out from cafés.

If Reseph weren't so scared and alone, Will thought sadly, he might find a bustling city scene like the one in Heatherfield pretty cool, especially compared to the scene in gloomy old Metamoor. But Reseph was a stranger to Will's world, and he was alone—and scared.

Will continued to be occupied with thoughts of the little boy. By now, he would be hungry. Perhaps he'd spot a bakery window display, piled high with croissants, cookies, and muffins. He'd forget for a moment to cower inside his burlap cloak. He'd put his scaly little hands on the plate glass and lick his lips hungrily, revealing tiny, pointed teeth.

Someone would emerge from the bakery—a child of the same height as Reseph. The child would be holding on to the hem of his mother's coat.

Reseph would spot the boy at the same time the boy laid his own shocked eyes on him. The kid would take in the vermilion stripes on Reseph's cheeks, the creature's stooped, animal-like posture, and bare, lizardlike feet.

Scared, Reseph would turn to dash off down the street. Just before he reached the corner, he'd hear the boy say to his mother, "Look, Mommy! It's one of Santa's elves!"

Reseph would have no idea what that meant. He would only feel more fear. He'd run, wide-eyed and stumbling, through a small park, only to end up on another busy street.

In a city crammed with Christmas shoppers, there would be no refuge except in an alley. Reseph would spot one of those dark corridors between two buildings and run for it as though he were running for his life.

Oblivious to the alley's puddles and scattered garbage, Reseph would crouch gratefully in a shadow.

Then, he'd spot a grate in the cement on the other side of the alley. Rumbling beneath the grate would be a subway tunnel, one that sent visible puffs of warm steam drifting into the air. Reseph would scramble over to the grate and stand on it, his six green toes curling with relief.

Reseph would spot the discarded flap of a cardboard box propped up by a garbage can. He'd curl up on the grate and pull the cardboard over himself as a blanket.

And then, Will thought with a small smile, he'd meet a different earthling—a puppy. Scared, homeless, and cold himself, the dog would curl up next to Reseph, rumbling with pleasure. Enjoying the shared warmth, boy and dog would fall asleep, until—

"Well, well, well! What do we have here?"

Will cringed as she imagined the rude awakening of Reseph and his furry friend—a couple of dogcatchers prowling the alleys for prey.

Instantly loyal and protective toward Reseph, the puppy would emerge from behind the cardboard and growl at the intruders. The men—equipped with leashes and nets—would laugh.

"Another two guests to be locked up," onc of the men would declare.

And *that's* why we're headed for the pound now, Will thought, tossing her glossy, red 'do.

To rescue Reseph and maybe even that puppy.

The girls stalked on in grim silence until they arrived at a tall, green, stucco wall bearing the sign *Municipal Dog Pound*.

"We're here!" Will announced.

She bit her lip and looked up at the wall, which was tall and forbidding. It was impossible to tell what lay behind it, unless, of course, one had the ability to fly!

"Ready, Hay Lin?" Will asked, turning to her flying friend.

"You bet!" Hay Lin said eagerly. With a graceful kick, she rose into the air. She bobbed for a moment at the top of the wall, peeking over it.

"Everything looks fine from up here," she called down. "There are a bunch of outdoor dog kennels. Totally bare, too. I don't even see any *dogfood* in there!"

"What about guards?" Will yelled up to Hay Lin.

Hay Lin shrugged and shook her head.

"I see an office on the other side of the complex," Hay Lin said. "The guards are probably in there, keeping out of this cold. Too bad that the puppies in those open kennels don't have the same luxury!" Hay Lin's face became contorted in disgust.

Will nodded.

"Pull us up!" she called to Hay Lin.

Will watched Hay Lin thrust her palm up. Then she felt her stomach lurch as her feet were swept off the ground. She floated upward like a bobbing feather. And, just like a feather, Will tumbled backward and sideways as she traveled.

I guess Hay Lin hasn't really mastered *stable* flight yet, she thought with a giggle.

Next to her, Taranee was floating through the air, too. She was upside down—and equally delighted by the sensation.

"This is fun!" she exclaimed.

Will glanced down at Irma and Cornelia, who were watching them float away.

"While we look for Reseph," Will called down to them, "you distract any dogcatchers on duty."

Irma nodded and winked at Will. Cornelia waved and called out, "Good luck!"

When Will, Hay Lin, and Taranee landed on the opposite side of the wall, Will looked around and gulped.

We're gonna need that luck! she thought. *This place is worse than a maze.*

The girls stared at a long row of kennels made of the same green stucco as the wall of the pound. Each kennel was accessible by a door—locked, of course.

The only way the girls could have gotten a peek inside any of the kennels would have been by floating up to view the space between the enclosure's roof and walls. Rather than a solid wall that might have kept the dogs warm, that opening was filled only by a chain-link fence. Will could see some of the steadily falling snow wafting through the windows.

"Let's get started," she whispered to her friends with a sigh.

Nodding, Hay Lin flew the three Guardians up to the space. They hovered there, looking down into the kennel. The light was so shadowy Will could barely see.

"Reseph?" she called softly. "Reseph? Are you there?"

There was no answer, but when Will's eyes adjusted to the gloom she could see that the enclosure held only a solitary dog. It was a mangy, white mutt with long, matted fur and a woebegone expression on its face. The dog was shivering pathetically in the cold.

"Aw," Hay Lin crooned sadly. "Hi, there, you cute little puppy, you."

Will wanted to comfort the sad, little dog, too. After all, she worked in a pet store. She hated to see an animal looking so bedraggled.

But she had a mission to lead. And clearly, she, Taranee, and Hay Lin were going to be searching for Reseph for a while.

That got Will just a *little* worried about the other portion of their team. Cornelia and Irma could barely make it through a joint study session without erupting into an argument. Could they be trusted to work together to fend off the guards?

Will couldn't help herself. She *had* to check up on the pair. Whispering to Taranee and Hay Lin that they should keep searching while she was gone, Will floated (with the help of Hay Lin) back down. She skulked around the corner of the kennel and stole down another long aisle of enclosures. Will gritted her teeth at the sound of barks and whimpers. She had to focus on her current mission.

Soon, she arrived at the pound's only

insulated building—a small office with frosty windows and a furnace humming against one of its walls.

Well, at least *somebody's* comfortable, Will thought drily. Inching closer to the building, Will put her face up to one of the windows. Sitting behind a disheveled desk was a pasty-faced man in a pale blue uniform. He was munching on a sandwich and watching a little TV set that was propped up on the corner of his desk. He looked bored to tears—until, that is, a couple of unusual visitors appeared at his door.

Will clapped a hand over her mouth to stifle a laugh as Irma flounced into the room, her Guardian wings fluttering flirtily.

"May we come in?" irma cooed, already standing in front of the guard's desk.

Cornelia glided into the room behind Irma. Her long, purple skirt fluttered out behind her. She batted her long eyelashes at the guard.

Stunned, the man dropped his sandwich on the floor.

"Uh, can I help you girls?" he asked.

Well, Will admitted to herself from her perch outside the window. It isn't every day two young women with *wings* walk into your office.

Not to mention young women with the flirting skills of Irma Lair and Cornelia Hale!

"I sure hope you can help us," Cornelia said in a silky voice. She leaned against the guard's desk and assumed a tragic expression. "We're looking for our dog. His name is Reginald." Will had to admit that Cornelia was giving Irma a run for her flirting money.

"He's little and white, with brown spots," Irma said.

Nodding awkwardly, the guard reached into a file drawer and hauled out a fat, grimy ledger. He began flipping through several pages of records.

"Hmmm," he said. Will noticed that a bit of shredded lettuce from his sandwich was dangling from his chin as he searched. Finally, he looked up at Irma.

"No," he said. "No Reginald. No white with brown spots here."

"Okay," Irma said, suddenly bending over to prop her elbows on the desk. She planted her chin on her fists, kicked one foot up behind her and breathed, "How about brown with white spots?"

"Huh?" the guard blurted out. "Are you

playing a joke on me?"

"Why do you say that?" Irma demanded, feigning shock. "I'm just trying to find my puppy!"

Will saw Cornelia—who was standing behind Irma—roll her eyes. Will could almost hear Cornelia's scoffing: What an actress!

To Will's surprise, Cornelia kept her mouth shut. She didn't scold Irma for being over the top in her behavior, or stamp her foot with impatience.

She did, however, wiggle her index finger, unleashing a stream of green magic, which in turn flipped a big stack of papers off the guard's file cabinet and straight into the air.

"Oh, my!" Irma said innocently. "Your paperwork is flying away!" Then she winked at Cornelia and gave her a thumbs-up.

Will felt a happy little thrill shimmer through her. Irma and Cornelia were a stellar team.

Will grinned as the guard cried, "Help!"

"Gee, that's a strong draft coming through that door," Irma said, putting a finger to her chin and pretending to be perplexed.

"It must happen a lot around this time of

year," Cornelia replied with a shrug.

Stifling another giggle, Will reassured herself that the coast was *definitely* clear and set out to resume her search.

She ducked away from the window and ran back to the row of kennels. About halfway down the line by the time she returned, Hay Lin and Taranee were peeking into another enclosure. When Will joined them, they shook their heads—still no Reseph.

They were about to head for the next kennel when Will heard a noise from a kennel at the end of the line. It was a cry of pain.

"Quiet," Will whispered to her friends. "Somebody's down there."

The Guardians floated silently down the aisle and paused outside the kennel's open door. She heard a man's voice sputtering irritably inside.

"The thing bit me!" the guy complained. "Well, by tomorrow morning, he won't be biting anymore."

"And then," said another man, "we'll see what kind of dog it really is!"

That's gotta be Reseph, Will thought. What else could possibly look strange to a dogcatcher? It had to be him!

Will gazed hopefully down the aisle toward the office.

Come on, Irma and Cornelia, she urged silently. *Do your thing.*

Like clockwork, another bellow, and a crash, for good measure, sounded from the guard's office.

"What's that baboon up to?" the first voice growled.

"Let's check it out," said the second.

Will and her friends ducked around the corner. When Will peeked out a moment later, she saw the two dogcatchers shambling toward the office.

"Now!" she urged Taranee and Hay Lin. Together, they darted through the door that the dogcatchers had carelessly left open. They peeked through the chain-link fence that stood between the door and the rest of the kennel. Cowering in the corner, next to a skinny, brown puppy, was a little creature with green skin, three-toed feet, and a ragged, Metamoorian cloak.

"Reseph!" Will sighed with relief. She smiled at the Metamoorian boy through the fence. "Come with us. We aren't going to hurt you." She tried to sound reassuring.

A simple blast of Will's magic popped the gate open. Taranee stepped into the kennel and held out her arms, and Reseph scrambled gratefully into them.

"Okay!" Will cried. She turned to run out the door. Taranee was right on her heels. They dashed down the row of kennels, heading for the doorway in the towering wall.

But Hay Lin was lagging behind.

"The poor puppies," she said. "I hate the terrible conditions they live in."

"Me, too," Will called back over her shoulder. "But there's no time to deal with it now. We've got to get Reseph out of here!"

"And fast!" Taranee said. Will saw her friend's arm tighten protectively around the little creature.

Hay Lin nodded.

But a moment later, she stopped and turned around.

She dashed back into one of the kennels.

"Hay Lin!" Will cried.

It was no use. Her friend had disappeared.

Will bit her lip. She remembered the last

time one of her friends had been left behind on a mission. Taranee had ended up trapped in Metamoor. That time, when Will had decided to put the mission first, rather than stopping for Taranee, she had done the right thing. Even Taranee had assured her of that.

I guess the Power of Five, Will thought, means trusting *all* of our instincts. And clearly, Hay Lin has a plan.

So Will grinned at Taranee and said, "Come on! She'll be all right."

Together, the girls pushed open the locked door and ran onto the sidewalk. While Reseph shivered in Taranee's arms, the Guardians hid behind a tree to see what would happen next. It was too tempting to see how the guards would react!

They didn't have to wait long! The guard tumbled out of the pound office, looking completely freaked out. He was tailed by the surly dogcatchers. One of them was still cradling the hand that Reseph had bitten.

"Would you mind telling us what you were up to?" he demanded of the guard. "And why you couldn't come give us a hand with that freaky, green dog?"

"W—well," the guard stuttered, with a wild look in his eyes. "It's just that everything in the room started flying around!"

"Uh-huh," the dogcatcher said drily. "Since when do things just start flying around without the help of wings?"

Suddenly, Cornelia and Irma appeared in the doorway behind the befuddled men. They looked as cool and breezy as ever.

"Mysterious flying," Cornelia quipped, glancing into the air above the dog pound. "Hmmm. I couldn't tell you for sure what's making that happen. But it does seem to be happening *a lot* around here."

The guards followed Cornelia's gaze up into the night sky. Will and Taranee did, too. Then everybody gasped.

A grinning Hay Lin was flying through the air, her long skirt fluttering. Flying all around her were dozens of dogs, yelping with joy and surprise. Hay Lin had liberated every bedraggled pup in the entire pound.

Will felt a surge of pride.

Could her friends be any cleverer? Or braver? Or . . . wittier? Especially Cornelia and Irma, who were leaving the guards with a few parting words of advice.

"Well, maybe we should get going," Cornelia said to Irma. "Wouldn't you say?"

"I'd say so," Irma quipped, running a hand through her bouncy, brown locks. Then she turned to the dumbstruck dogcatchers and winked. "Have a nice evening, fellas. And if I can give you a piece of advice . . ."

Irma pointed at the departing Hay Lin and her magical menagerie.

"Try," Irma giggled, "not to think about all of this too hard!"

BY TOMORROW MORNING YOU WON'T BE BITING ANYMORE!
AND THEN WE'LL SEE WHAT KIND OF MUTT YOU REALLY ARE!
CRASH
BAM
HELP!
GEE! THAT'S A STRONG DRAFT COMING THROUGH THAT DOOR.
IT HAPPENS AROUND THIS TIME OF YEAR!
NOW!
WHAT'S THAT BABOON UP TO?
COME WITH US, RESEPH! WE AREN'T GOING TO HURT YOU!
POOR PUPS! LOOK AT THE TERRIBLE CONDITIONS THEY MAKE YOU LIVE IN. . . .
THERE'S NO TIME FOR THAT NOW, HAY LIN! WE'VE GOT TO GET OUT OF HERE!
AND FAST!
HAY LIN!

WOULD YOU MIND TELLING ME WHAT YOU'RE UP TO, AND WHY YOU COULDN'T COME AND GIVE US A HAND?
WELL . . . IT'S JUST THAT . . . EVERYTHING IN THE ROOM SUDDENLY STARTED FLYING AROUND!
AND SINCE WHEN DO THINGS FLY?
I COULDN'T TELL YOU FOR SURE. . . .
. . . BUT IT SEEMS TO BE HAPPENING A LOT AT THIS POUND!
MUNICIPAL DOG POUND
GASP!
ARGH!
MAYBE WE SHOULD GET GOING, HUH?
I'D SAY SO! HAVE A NICE EVENING, FELLAS, AND IF I CAN GIVE YOU A PIECE OF ADVICE . . .
TRY NOT TO THINK ABOUT IT!

EPILOGUE. SHEFFIELD INSTITUTE, THE NEXT DAY
YOUR TEST RESULTS WERE DISAPPOINTING, TO SAY THE LEAST.
THERE WAS ONE EXCEPTION. ONE GRADE WAS SURPRISINGLY POSITIVE: IRMA LAIR'S.
HUH?
READ ALOUD TO YOUR CLASSMATES WHAT YOU WROTE, IRMA. CLASS, LISTEN TO WHAT FRENCH REALLY SOUNDS LIKE.
YES!
A
CORNELIA! WILL! I'M A GENIUS!
JE SUIS GENIALE, MERVEILLEUSE, EXTRAORDINAIRE!
SHE PASSED HER TEST!
WAY TO GO, IRMA!
IF THAT'S THE CASE, THEN THERE'S A TRYOUT WAITING FOR YOU!
ALL RIGHT! I LOVE THIS SCHOOL!

AND SO . . .
DON'T MOVE A MUSCLE!
OUCH! YOU STABBED ME!
BUT YOU MOVED! YOU MAY BE THE RED DRAGON, BUT YOU'RE REALLY SHORT ON PATIENCE!
LOOK WHO'S HERE. . . . THE GRUMPERS!
GOOD! I WAS WAITING FOR THEM!
GIRLS, IT'S SO NICE TO SEE YOU!
WHAT'S SHE DOING? WHY IS SHE EVEN TALKIN TO THEM?
CORNELIA HAS **QUESTIONABLE** TASTE IN FRIENDS!
THOSE SLIMEBALLS! I'M REALLY HAPPY THEY DIDN'T MAKE IT THROUGH THE TRYOUTS!

ANOTHER PROBLEM SOLVED!
ARE YOU STILL TALKING TO HOSE CREEPS?
CALM DOWN! ALL I DID WAS TELL THEM ABOUT THE PARTY.
PARTY? WHAT PARTY?
THE COSTUME PARTY AFTER THE SHOW. IT'S A PARTY TO INAUGURATE THE NEW GYM!
I TOLD THEM NOT TO TELL ANYBODY! IT'S BY INVITATION ONLY. . . . AND THEY PROMISED TO KEEP IT A SECRET.
BUT . . . BUT . . . BUT . . .
THERE'S NO PARTY AFTER THE SHOW!
OH, WE KNOW THAT. . . .
BUT THE GRUMPERS DON'T!
A! HA! HA! HA!

GRRRR!
GRR
HEY THERE! FEROCIOUS LITTLE FELLOW, AREN'T YOU?
GROWWL
WHERE ARE YOU GOING?
YAP YAP YAP
SO WHERE DID YOU COME FROM? WHERE'S YOUR OWNER?
YAP YAP YAP
COME HERE, TRIXIE!
THE SHOW'S ABOUT TO START! GET BACK TO YOUR SEAT. . . .

RESEPH!
IT'S STARTING!
"WHAT WILL YOU TELL YOUR GRANDCHILDREN IN YEARS TO COME?"
"OF MAGICAL ADVENTURES IN UNKNOWN LANDS?"
"OF AFFECTION THAT BRINGS TOGETHER DIFFERENT PEOPLE?"
"OF FRIENDSHIP THAT UNITES YOU FOREVER?"
CLAP CLAP CLAP
CLAP CLAP CLAP
CLAP CLAP CLAP
CLAP CLAP CLAP

"OR MAYBE . . . OF THE WORST SNOWSTORM IN THE LAST 150 YEARS?"
HAPPY HOLIDAYS!
TO BE CONTINUED . . .